MW01633702

AVENGING JULIE (SPECIAL FORCES: OPERATION ALPHA)

GUARDIANS OF HOPE

KD MICHAELS

Dear Readers,

Welcome to the Special Forces: Operation Alpha Fan-Fiction world!

If you are new to this amazing world, in a nutshell the author wrote a story using one or more of my characters in it. Sometimes that character has a major role in the story, and other times they are only mentioned briefly. This is perfectly legal and allowable because they are going through Aces Press to publish the story.

This book is entirely the work of the author who wrote it. While I might have assisted with brainstorming and other ideas about which of my characters to use, I didn't have any part in the process or writing or editing the story.

I'm proud and excited that so many authors loved my characters enough that they wanted to write them into their own story. Thank you for supporting them, and me!

READ ON!
Xoxo
Susan Stoker

"What the hell did you do to him?" Detective Laura 'Red' Pratt asked her teammate, Detective Cheryl Diesel.

"The hell if I know. Just walked into the room and his ass started flapping." Diesel shrugged.

"Just walked into the room, huh?" Detective Lindsey 'Ice' Raso asked, walking into the interrogation room.

"No, I just talked to him, didn't lay a damn finger on his dumbass. Thought Tex said this fool was a jarhead?" Diesel said in defense.

"He's not Siri, you dopehead." Detective Kaitey Rameriez said, from behind Raso.

"He's definitely not a smart one, that's for sure." Detective Renee York said, standing next to Pratt.

"Not even semi smartphone probability. I thought Marine's had to have a high IQ?" Diesel asked the group of women standing with her.

"Hell, he's not even flip phone material." Detective Tarilyn 'Taz' Cortez responded, joining the group.

"What in the ever-loving hell, did you guys do to the suspect?" Captain Kathryn Irby asked, joining Alpha Squad in the interrogation observation room.

Diesel walked over to their suspect, Bobby Jenkins, who had been delivered to the team in San Diego two days ago. When the Delta team in Texas couldn't get any answers from him after going a few rounds, they had him delivered to Diesel, Alpha Squad's top interrogator.

"Do we know what Ghost and his men did to him during their interrogation?" Raso asked as she watched Diesel check the unconscious man's pulse.

"Loud music, sleep deprivation, knee cap replacement and a few rib relocations." Diesel answered.

"Ah, so they did the same thing that happens to them when they go through spec ops training?" Raso stated with a chuckle.

"Um, Diez, is that supposed to happen when you check someone's pulse?" Rameriez asked, trying hard not to laugh.

"The fuck?" Diesel yelled as she jumped back out of the way, while looking down to where Rameriez pointed at the same time.

"Hey Diesel, don't forget to check it's pulse too," Pratt said, laughing.

"Fuck you, Pratt. I'm not touching his little prick." Diesel said, moving back away from the suspect on the floor. "Stupid fucker is still alive, for now."

"So why did he pass out?" Rameriez asked Diesel.

"Probably because he hit the end of the road." Diesel grumbled.

"Did you even start interrogating him?" Cortez asked.

"No, I just got him about ten minutes ago. It wasn't even Ghost or his team that delivered the jackass either, was some other team." Diesel answered, clearly annoyed.

"Well, let's wake his ass up." Pratt stated, starting to step forward.

"We will, you back your pregnant ass back." Raso said, blocking Pratt from entering the room.

"Blah blah blah, bitch got jokes today." Pratt fired back.

"Red, your ass is eight months pregnant right now, shut it. Highlander's still pissed about Texas,

I'm not adding to that shit storm with you getting close to this jerkoff." Raso said, reminding Pratt of their fiasco in Texas.

"Yeah, tell me about it, I'm the one going without sex right now." Pratt grumbled.

"I thought you guys worked that stuff out already?" York asked in surprise. "What do you mean *you're* the one going without? He's not getting any either if you're not!"

"Nuh uh, he's using his hands, fucking Rosie Palmer and her bitchass sisters." Pratt mumbled. "I thought we'd worked it out too. I think it's punishment because I talked to his mom about the no sex issue, then took her advice which got me nookie. I, uh, also told her about my fears with this pregnancy. His mom apparently told his dad, who then called and reamed his tail out." Pratt shrugged.

"You told his mom he wasn't putting out?" Cortez asked, laughing at the same time. "That probably doesn't help with the stress level, especially all this b.s. you're now going through with your ex-husband is putting you through."

"What b.s.?" Captain Irby asked, looking between the women, sounding annoyed.

"It's nothing, really, Captain. Just some crap that Jon is wanting to start now because Cody doesn't want to do his visitations. Plus, we sent him paperwork, via the attorney, asking him to surrender his parental rights so that Highlander can adopt him legally." Pratt told her Captain.

"Since when did he do visitation? So, it boils down to the fact that you're not single anymore, you've found a real man who is there for you and your son and he loses that dream of you eventually needing his sorry ass? Have you told the Lt?" Captain Irby asked Pratt.

"Um, no ma'am. I'm not going to either. The only reason Cortez knows is because the asshole and the twit he's married to were at the diner when we went to pick up lunch for the team the other day." Pratt informed the group.

"That jerk seriously downgraded that's for sure." Cortez responded.

"Well, he does have his mom's dick." York chuckled, causing the group of women to laugh.

"Laura, if he gives you any major problems, let me know. No if's, ands or buts, got it?" Captain Irby asked in a serious tone.

"Yes ma'am." Pratt said quickly.

"Alright, ladies, wake this piece of shit up and lets get this interrogation started. You're now on black out status. Do whatever it takes to get him to talk."

Captain Irby ordered the group. "Detective Pratt, with me in observation. Don't think I haven't forgotten about your condition, it's staring me in the face."

"Damn it!" Pratt said, as she stomped before making her way towards the observation area with the Captain, causing the others to laugh.

Three hours, several busted ear drums, thousands of curse words and a medical ride later, Alpha Squad was no closer to finding out where Gerry Lidell was or who hired the group that had ambushed them in Texas, at the same time kidnapping Emily Fletcher, Cheyenne Cooper, a package that Alpha Squad was transporting and Detective Cortez. It was painfully obvious to the team that Gerry Lidell didn't confide in his cousin about who the client was. The team was back to square one.

"Damn it, I really don't want to be the one to tell Wolf or Ghost that we got nothing." Pratt grouched to the group.

"Well, on the bright side, they have more advanced training than we do, and they got no where with this asshole either." York said, looking around the room.

"Well, we do know that Lidell doesn't give a rats

ass about his cousin. There's been no attempts to rescue the loser." Cortez said, lost in thought.

"That's because word went out, via the media and military channels, that Bobby Jenkins was killed, along with the other three bodies that were taken out. No one has come to identify or claim any of the bodies either." Sgt. Helen Brocard said, joining the group.

"Well, that could explain it all ther." Raso quipped.

"Detective Pratt, do you know if there's been any more attempts made on the women?" Captain Irby asked.

"Not so far, ma'am. The teams and Delta have pretty much stayed in constant touch to make sure nothing has gone on separate. More than likely, Lidell went underground to regroup and lick his wounds." Pratt answered, rubbing her belly.

"Well they definitely got some wounds. We pretty much took out the group they hired, and four of their own." Ramereiz said with a smile.

"Okay, Pratt, I want you, Raso, and Cortez to take Tammy out to look for her prom dress. Here's the name and address of the shop you can go and look around at. It's a second-hand store, but they have great quality clothing." Captain Irby told the three women.

"On it. I'm so glad that Tammy decided to go to her senior prom. I was afraid she'd chicken out after last week." York said.

"Yeah, I think it helped when Cortez and Diesel went to the school to put the fear of God into those little bitches." Pratt said, laughing at the memory.

"Amen! I've got no problem putting those skankellas in their places. Tammy has come too dang far for sluts like that to ruin it for her. All because the captain of the high school football team got ass hurt that Tammy wouldn't go out with him? Let me hear that shithead mess with her again, they won't have a captain anymore since his ass will be in traction." Cortez growled out.

"We're still going to chaperone right?" Rameriez asked the group.

"Yep. Highlander told his team about what happened as well. Apparently, Wolf's team was working out with them and heard about it as well, so both teams have offered to be her prom date." Pratt told the group.

"Aren't Wolf and his team all married?" Diesel asked, scratching her head.

"Yeah, but they told the wives about Tammy's

situation and they all agreed. Caroline called me and said they all donated their husbands for the cause." Pratt said, shaking her head and laughing.

"Donated their husband to the cause?" Raso laughed. "I knew I loved those women for a reason."

The women of Alpha Squad, a task force that goes after human traffickers in Riverside County, California, were momma hens when it came to victims they rescued. The group kept in touch with a large majority of the victims they rescued through the years, helping them out in any way possible, so that they could get back on their feet and become productive members of society.

"Let's go check out 'My Sister's Closet'. Caroline is always raving about that place. They apparently have rich people clothes at poor people prices." Pratt told Cortez and Raso.

"Nice, let's go pick up little bits, then we can rock and roll." Cortez said, heading for the door. "Shotgun!"

"Rock, paper, scissors on who's driving." Raso challenged Pratt.

"Bitch, get in the back seat. It's my damn car." Pratt said, laughing, as she walked away.

"Can you even fit behind the wheel?" Raso challenged. "Bet you have to let Highlander drive with that belly."

"Yeah, his ass drives his damn truck." Pratt fired over her shoulder. "Do you let every peckerhead you put out with drive your car?"

"Hell to the no, I don't let no man drive my car. Have you lost your brain cells with this pregnancy?" Raso asked defending herself.

"Bet you let Pats drive your car." Pratt challenged her coworker.

"Oh, hell no! Have you ever ridden with that asshole?" Raso asked Pratt. "I'm still pissed at you for tricking me into driving with him the other day."

"He still tries to drive on the wrong side of the road too huh?" Pratt asked, hiding her laugher behind a cough.

"You're pure evil woman! That kid is going to come out with horns and a pitchfork." Raso said, sitting in back and crossing her arms over her chest.

"Hurry the hell up! You two are slower than my grandma with a bad hip." Cortez groaned, stomping her foot.

"High school much?" Raso mumbled back.

"You're just pissed because I called shotgun first and Red here won't let you drive." Cortez responded with sass.

"Both of you shut the hell up and put your seat belts on." Pratt yelled, starting her brand-new car.

"Bitch" Cortez and Raso said in union.

"You ho's are just jealous of my new ride." Pratt challenged.

For an early wedding present, Pratt's fiancé, Lieutenant Joseph 'Highlander' MacLeod, got her a brand new royal blue 2018 Dodge Charger that had state of the art features and additions. The modifications allowed Pratt to use the vehicle for both work and personal needs. Highlander took his family's safety seriously. What Pratt loved the most about the car, was the black and blue interior, the rear facing camera for backing up the car, as specialized camera on the dashboard that allowed her to facetime with Highlander or Cody when she wasn't home.

"Damn skippy I'm jealous. I should get one too for putting up with his brothers annoying ass." Raso said, pouting in the back seat.

"Oh, shut up already. I can't wait for you two to stop dancing around and just start bumping uglies already." Pratt said, rolling her eyes. Pratt and Cortez laughed when Raso flipped her off.

"On a more serious note, Captain has called a meeting for the team tomorrow morning. Any idea what it's about?" Cortez asked the other two women.

"No clue. I'm wondering if it's about Texas? I mean that's all we've been focused on lately, aside from our normal case load. A lot of our stuff has been handed over to Bravo Squad, to give us breathing room." Raso answered, looking out the back-seat window.

"Maybe Delta found out more information than we are aware of?" Pratt said, shrugging, as she drove onto the street where they were to pick up their package.

"That whole issue in Texas was a nightmare." Cortez stated, staring out the window.

"For you more than the rest of us." Raso said, quietly.

"I knew what I was doing, the other two women, they were in over their heads, but held it together and remained strong. Sophie was my main concern." Cortez stated, matter-of-factly.

"What keeps biting my craw is why only Bolden was killed. If they were shooting to take us out, why not kill all of us? Don't get me wrong guys, I'm glad we're all still alive, but it just didn't make any sense that she was the only one killed by the sniper fire. Raso, you and Brocard were both hit in the shoulder and stomach. Yeah, it could have killed you, but it didn't. Bolden was killed with a head shot. Why didn't they take out all of us like they did when they blew up the other cars? That's why none of this is making any sense to me." Pratt told the two women she fought and bled for.

"That's been on all of our minds, Red. Sgt. Brocard and Captain Irby have been beating the drums for answers. Sheriff Phillips has been going into meetings like crazy, even so far as to have meetings with some of the brass in the military to work side by side with them. We all want answers, us, the SEALs, and the Delta boys." Raso confirmed.

"It's pissing all of us off on how long it's taken to get anything dealt with. Hell, Texas was three freaking months ago." Cortez said on a sigh.

Three months prior, Alpha Squad had been caught in the middle of a full-scale attempt to kidnap Caroline, Fiona, Cheyenne, Emily and Rayne, Navy SEAL and Delta Force wives, while they were out shopping in Killeen, Texas. Because Alpha Squad happened to be in the wrong place at the right time, they were able to fight back which resulted in only Cheyenne and Emily being taken, along with Detective Cortez and a human trafficking victim they had been transporting to a safe house near the base, Sophie.

Their new recruit, Detective Jessica Bolden, had

been killed instantly with a shot to the head while Sgt. Brocard and Detective Raso sustained serious injuries from two bullet wounds each. The remaining four team members had worked side by side with the SEALs who were in Texas on vacation visiting their Delta Force friends, and Delta Force to rescue the four women. When they rescued the women, it only turned into a nightmare they weren't expecting, a nightmare they found out, when the smoke cleared, was far from over. Three months later, they were still no closer to finding out who the mastermind and money man was in hiring a group of AWOL SEALs and former Special Forces operatives to kidnap the wives of both teams.

CHAPTER 2

The bell above the door to 'My Sister's Closet' dinged, alerting Julie Hurt to new customers. Coming out of the back, she saw Caroline, Cheyenne and Summer laughing, with Mozart, Wolf and Dude in tow behind them. She waived at the group, smiling, and walked out to greet them.

"Hi, everyone. If you need anything, just let me know. We had some new stuff come in this week." Julie told the group.

"Hi Julie, thanks! I can't wait to see what you have new. How is everything?" Caroline Steel asked.

"It's all good. Staying busy. How about you?" Julie asked.

"Doing great. I hear congratulations are in order?" Caroline asked, smiling.

"I take it Patrick told the guys huh?" Julie said, smiling big.

"Yes, ma'am. Commander Hurt's been passing out cigars. He's on cloud nine." Matthew 'Wolf' Steel stated, with a laugh, as he turned around when the bell over the door rang.

"Hi, welcome to 'My Sister's Closet'." Julie said to the group walking in.

"Oh, my goodness. Laura Renee MacLeod, are you in uniform?" Caroline asked, attempting to scold Pratt.

"It's still Pratt, Caroline. Wedding hasn't happened yet." Pratt said laughing. "And yes, I am still in uniform. Will be until the Dr puts me on maternity leave or the water breaks, which ever happens first. Mom."

"Looks like you could pop any day now." Cheyenne said, walking over to hug the three women.

"Three and a half weeks left. Can't come soon enough. I forgot this part of my pregnancy with Cody." Pratt said, smiling at the memory. "Praying I go early, but, doubting it. Cody was two weeks late. If this munchkin is anything like his or her brother, then they may make me wait too."

"Highlander treating you right red head?" Wolf asked, hugging Pratt.

"Define right?" Cortez asked on a snort.

"Shut it bone head." Pratt said, elbowing her teammate. "And to answer your question, no. Tried to have a little noogie last night since you know, sex is supposed to help, and the bastard made me sleep alone while he went and slept on the couch. He's lucky I didn't stab his ass. Can I borrow your basement for a few weeks?" Pratt asked Wolf, batting her eyelashes and giving the puppy dog eyes.

"Sure" Caroline quickly replied.

"Trying to get me killed babe?" Wolf asked at the same time.

"Fine!" Pratt said, dragging out the n. "I'll move his stuff into your basement.

Raso and Cortez laughed. "You couldn't last one night without him in the house, knowing he's not deployed." Cortez retorted.

"Wanna bet?" Pratt challenged with a straight face.

"She would, just to prove a point to you two." Dude laughed, pulling Pratt into a hug as well. "Red, do you want me and Mozart to talk to him? We've been in his shoes."

"Yeah and nearly got beaten to a bloody pulp too." Summer said quietly.

Pratt sighed, cutting her chuckle short. "Dude, he doesn't even listen to Doc, Doc's wife or his parents. Even the Dr has told him sex is safe. Just makes me feel like I'm a beached whale that he can't stand to be around or wishes I was someone else."

"I'm kicking your ass later!" Raso growled at her best friend, getting pissed.

"I'll join in." Wolf, Dude and Mozart all said at the same time.

"Guys, back off. She's getting enough shit from her fucking mother, former step-sisters and her ex-husband. Doesn't help when the squid pulls away too." Cortez said, defending Pratt.

"What the hell are you talking about?" Mozart and Caroline both asked together, confusion in their expressions.

"Her twatmuffin mother filed a complaint with I.A. two weeks ago against Pratt, then last week filed one against Highlander with his command. She claims they were harassing her and made her fear for her life. The late step-mother's two twits are trying to sue her for their mother's death. They also sent fake photoshop photos to the house of Highlander with another woman." Cortez said, ratting out Pratt.

"What the fuck?" Wolf, Dude, and Mozart all said at the same time, looking at each other.

"What woman? When he's at the base he's always with one of the guys or us, at the range, PT or in his office with the door wide open. He doesn't even go out for lunch unless one of us is with him. I know there's been no other female. When he leaves, he goes straight home since he's the one usually picking up Cody or doing something with Cody in the evenings." Dude stated, defending Highlander.

"Wait a minute, is that why you two were fighting last night when I came over to drop off the files and pick up the others?" Raso asked, concerned.

"Partially. His team is grounded until further notice. Well, at least until their review is done. Supposedly, the attorney my mother hired has claimed the teams weren't sanctioned to be on the op when we first met, that they used excessive force." Pratt said quietly, walking away to help Tammy look for her dress.

"That's it, I'm talking to him. His ass better not be blaming her for this fiasco." Dude said, clearly upset.

"That op was a black out, how did this attorney get any information on it?" Wolf asked out loud.

"My thinking, he can't get any information. Probably got told no comment, and his dumbass is taking it as a no." Cortez said, stating her own opinion on the situation.

"They weren't arguing about the grounding. It was about his whereabouts at work or after work when I got there. I don't think she told him about the photos." Raso said, looking towards Pratt.

"Her mother is getting advice from someone since this shit started two weeks ago." Cortez said.

"Hold on, when did her stepmother die?" Caroline asked the two women.

"It would be two years ago, when we did a raid on a compound they were held up in. It was when we handled Russell's case when he was accused of murdering his mother." Raso stated, for clarification.

"And they are just now…" Wolf said, stopping himself as he pulled out his phone, walking away. Ten minutes later, he walked back to the group. "Tex is looking into some things for us."

"Don't kill Highlander guys." Cortez said. "Give him a chance, he may be doing the same thing she is, holding a lot of the shit going on to his chest thinking he's protecting her."

"No promises, but if he shows remorse, we may

be lenient." Dude said in a deadly quiet voice. "Where did she go?"

"She's helping Tammy with finding a dress for prom. We're escorting her this year." Cortez said, looking around.

"Oh, that's right, Tammy is the kid that High-lander was telling everyone about." Wolf said, looking towards Pratt and Tammy were. "We plan on being there with everyone, in case there's any issues."

Cortez nodded and thanked the group, waived at Julie and walked towards where Pratt and Tammy were standing. Pratt started to turn around and say something when loud pops sounded, glass shattered everywhere, screams went out, and she went flying back into the clothes rack.

Caroline, Cheyenne, Summer and Julie were pushed to the ground by the men, using their bodies to protect the four women, while yelling at the other four to get down. Raso and Cortez withdrew their weapons and crawled to the door, away from the window to return fire, giving the men time to get the women to safety.

Dude and Mozart crawled over to Pratt since she was the only one not moving along with the rest of the group. "Red, are you okay? Talk to me." Dude said, sounding concerned.

"I would if you shushed damn it. Shit, that hurt." Pratt said, trying to catch her breath.

"Where did you get hit?" Mozart asked, going into medic mode.

"Arm and abdomen area. My vest caught the abdomen area, thank goodness. Arm burns like a mofo though. Where's Tammy and the others?" Pratt asked, trying to sit up, but falling back as searing pain gripped her abdomen.

"She's behind the counter with Caroline. Raso and Cortez are covering the front until we can get you to safety. Shit, Highlander is going to be pissed when he finds out you're hit." Dude remarked, looking Pratt over for more injuries.

"No, he won't." Pratt panted, breathing through the pain.

"Don't make me tan your ass." Dude warned, with a mock growl.

"Don't threaten me with a good time then, Duuuude." Pratt fired back, causing both men to chuckle at her attempt to sound okay.

"How's the baby?" Mozart asked, dressed her arm wound.

"Kicking up a storm right now. That's how I

know it's a girl." Pratt said on a groan, as more pain hit her abdomen. "Shit that one hurt."

"What?" Mozart and Dude asked in union.

"Just the pain from when Mozart tied the damn thing around my arm." Pratt said, hiding the fact she was having pain in the lower abdomen.

"Called it in, back up is on the way. Pratt, your ass is going to the hospital when the ambulance gets here, or I'll have Dude hog tie your ass and drag you there." Raso said, making sure there was no room for argument.

"Shots are coming from the roof across the street and the black SUV that's parked catty corner to us." Cortez said from her spot by the window.

"Mozart get the women into the very back room. Cortez, you're with me and Dude. Raso, I want you to guard the back-entrance door in case someone decides to try and come through the back way. Let's take these assholes down, we need to get Pratt to the hospital ASAP. The ambulance can't get in here if they are still shooting at us." Wolf said, taking control of the chaos.

Mozart and Dude helped Pratt up from the floor, escorting her and the small group of women into Julie's office area. Raso rushed to the back-storage area to cover the door, while Wolf and Cortez held watch on the front area, waiting for their unknown shooters to breach.

"We need to get Pratt to the hospital, *now*. She was hit twice trying to protect Tammy when things went down. She's trying to hide it, but she's having contractions. There's blood her pants, on her upper thigh. Mozart thinks the placenta may have been torn from the wall. Mozart got the bleeding in the arm to stop, but he's worried about the contractions and bleeding." Dude informed Wolf and Cortez, with concern in his voice.

"Shit, she's not due for another three and a half weeks, granted, if she did have the baby now, they would both be ok, but either way, Highlander is going to be pissed the fuck off. You two are going to have to deal with him. His alpha shit has gotten worse since Texas." Cortez told the two men.

"We got her back, Cortez. We'll deal with Highlander. Let's just focus on these tangos so we can get the fuck out of here." Wolf said, looking out the window. "They've gone quiet, but I highly doubt they've left. Keep an eye out, something tells me this isn't over yet."

Soon as Wolf made that statement, two men cautiously stepped through the broken window, guns raised, trying to be quiet when they stepped on the broken glass scattered all over the floor of the store. The crunching of the glass under the tango's feet, loud in the eerie silence, giving a false sense of security.

Wolf, Dude and Cortez slid down into a crouch behind a rack of clothing, making sure they had enough view of the tangos as they advanced into the store. Seconds after the second tango stepped through the window, a loud bang broke through the silence, coming from the back-storage room.

The two tangos sprung into action, running towards the back where the noise came from, totally oblivious to the three figures hidden in the racks. Wolf stuck his foot out, tripping one tango as Dude jumped from his position to tackle the second one to the ground. Cortez jumped up and ran to the back room where Raso was in a struggle with a third tango who tried to sneak into through the back door. Both women quickly subdued the bad guy, cuffing his hands behind his back and patting him down.

Cortez and Raso drug their tango to the front, by his upper arms, letting his lower body drag on the ground, laying him next to the other two tangos who were knocked out with their hands zip tied behind their back. Raso looked at the men with a quirked eye brow when she saw the zip ties, smirking and shaking her head when they shrugged, giving no explanation. Wolf took a photo of all three men, then sent a text to Tex with a request to help identify them before the police got there to take them away. Several minutes later, Wolf and Mozart were helping the medics load Pratt into the ambulance, Caroline climbing into the back of the ambulance with her, after giving Wolf a quick kiss.

"She's going to have a cow that one of us has to drive her baby." Raso said to Cortez.

"Is it bad that I'm willing to toss you for the privilege?" Cortez laughed, pulling out a quarter from her pocket.

Wolf and Dude laughed, shaking their heads. "Don't scratch her baby. She will pop that kid out, then kill you two." Wolf said, laughing at Cortez and Raso as they flipped the coin.

"Well, they do have a problem no matter who wins that coin toss." Mozart said, with a shit eating grin on his face from the sidelines.

"Why's that?" Cortez asked, doing a happy dance when she won the coin toss.

"Well, she gave *me* the keys and told me or Dude to drive the car to the hospital." Mozart said with an evil grin, holding up the keys so they dangled in front of Raso and Cortez.

"That heifer." Raso grumbled, causing everyone to laugh.

"Have you guys called Joe yet?" Summer asked. She and a few of the other wives had a thing about calling the SEALs by their real name instead of their call signs.

"Shit, this is one call I'm dreading." Wolf said as he pulled out his phone. "Mozart, you and Dude go ahead and take the others on to the hospital. I'll meet up with you all after I call Highlander. Let Caroline know I'll be there soon as I call him."

CHAPTER 3

Highlander walked into the waiting room thirty minutes later, looking haggard and beaten. Trailing behind Highlander, Highlander's SEAL teammates came in to join the melee of waiting for news on their team leader's heart and soul. Alpha Squad, Captain Irby, Sheriff Phillips, Wolf, his team, their wives – minus Jessyka who took the kids, Commander Hurt, Julie and Pratt's brother Dominick were gathered around waiting for word on Pratt.

"What the hell happened? Has there been any word on Laura?" Lt. Joe 'Highlander' MacLeod asked the room.

"That's the million-dollar question Lander. Several tangos opened fire from across the street and the rooftop into the store." Wolf informed the irate SEAL.

"I knew I should have pushed harder for the fucking maternity leave." Highlander bellowed, clearly upset and worried.

"Oh, hell naw! You are seriously not fucking going there you, Scottish bastard. Any one of these women could have been hit. Red just happened to be there and did her job protecting a civilian the best that she could. She is going to be fine and you're scrowly ass isn't going to take that away from her. Between your sorry ass and her fucking family, I'm surprised she hasn't been put on bed room already." Diesel screamed at Highlander, losing her cool.

"What the hell do ye mean by me and her fucking family?" Highlander asked in confusion.

"Diesel, what do you mean by my family? Laura hasn't said anything to me the family." Dominick asked in equal confusion.

"Shit" Wolf mumbled.

"Oh shit" Raso and Cortez whispered in union.

"Damn it, Diesel, she didn't want him to know about this shit." York whispered loudly.

"Know what?" Dominick Pratt, Laura's older brother, demanded, clearly losing his cool with the women.

"Know what lasses?" Highlander asked, trying to temper his growing anger and concern.

Wolf sighed, stepping forward. "Joe, apparently her mother and the stepmother's two daughters have been causing her some issues."

"They aren't the only ones." Cortez mumbled.

"Son of a bitch!" Dominick said at the same time.

"What do ye mean they aren't the only ones?" Highlander asked Cortez.

"Damn it." Cortez whispered.

Dude coughed and stepped up beside Wolf. "As Wolf was saying, apparently her mother and former step-sisters filed a complaint, causing Pratt to be placed under I.A. investigation, and she's also being sued by the step-sisters in the death of their mother."

"Those bitches." Dominick said, punching the wall.

"Son, I take it you didn't know about this either?" Sheriff Phillips asked Dominick.

"No sir, she never told me, which has me upset. Doesn't she realize I would have backed her up on this?" Dominick asked Alpha Squad.

"That's why she didn't want you knowing about it." Captain Irby told the room. "She didn't want to put a target on your back where these women were concerned. So far, they've only focused on her and she knows the Sheriff and I have her back on this. The department hired an attorney to defend her in this situation and we're supporting her 110%."

"Why didn't she tell me about this shite?" Highlander asked the group.

"Like you told her about the fact your team was grounded until further notice?" Rameriez challenged the Scottish SEAL.

"What?" Sheriff Phillips asked in confusion.

"And you turning her away last night didn't help the other shit they tried either." Raso let out of the bag.

"What other shite?" Highlander asked, clearly confused.

Cortez looked at Raso, then Highlander, then Dominick then back at Highlander on a sigh. "Just before you got home yesterday, a large envelope was delivered to the house. Inside the envelope was a set of photos that were clearly photoshopped, once we had them analyzed this morning. The photos showed you out with another woman over the last couple of months in intimate settings. Dates that show when you were supposedly deployed or at work."

"Shite, that's why she asked the questions she did

last night. Why didn't she just show me the photos?" Highlander asked.

"Ma'am, if you can get me those photos, I can put her mind at ease and verify the deployment dates. I'm not going to lie for my men." Commander Hurt said, joining in the conversation. "I can also have them analyzed further, by Tex, and see if we can't find out who sent them to her. I'm not going to lie about something like that for these men. That's something I don't approve of."

"I'll get the photos for you to be able to see who's doing it. But the dates don't need to be verified. She already knew they were fake. While she doesn't feel very attractive as a pregnant woman right now, she knows he wasn't cheating on her or lying to her."

"What the hell? Laura is the most beautiful pregnant woman I have ever met. I love my lass more than anything on this planet." Highlander said, at a loss for once.

"Let's get back to the real issue here. Lt, I thought you weren't going to tell her about us being grounded or that there was a review of the Russell issue?" Doc asked.

"He didn't." Cortez confirmed. "But she felt he blamed her for it when he went to sleep on the couch last night."

"What? No, I went to sleep on the couch last night because the cold fucking shower didn't help cool down the need I have for her." Highlander said loudly, his agitation ramping up.

"Highlander didn't tell her." York said, sighing as she joined the circle. "She found out when she ran into one of her mother's old biddie friends last week when we ran to the store for some stuff. The old bat confronted her in the middle of the isle. That's how she found out about the inquiry into you and your team." York confessed to Highlander and the rest of the group.

"She never told me." Highlander said, deflating.

"Any word on those tangos that attacked the store and who or what they were after?" Doc asked the group.

"No. I took a photo of each of them and sent it to Tex before the local police arrived and took them away. They aren't talking to anyone." Wolf said, shaking his head.

"They aren't talking to anyone, like Wolf said. We do know, from their tattoos, they are part of a local gang. We've reached out to the gang unit to see if they can help us identify these idiots. They were clearly hired out, but we don't know by who." York confirmed for everyone.

As York finished her statement, a tall middle-aged man, who looked like he was ready for a long nap walked into the waiting room. "I'm looking for the family of Detective Laura Pratt?"

"That's us sir. I'm her fiancée Joe, this is her brother Dominick. How is she?" Highlander asked, worried and sick to his stomach.

"I'm here to get you. Ms. Pratt is asking for you. We've tried everything we can to stop the bleeding, but the placenta detached itself from the uterine wall, so we have no choice but to do an emergency c-section and deliver the baby. She won't allow the nurse to give her anything without you there." The doctor informed Highlander.

"Is the baby going to be ok, being delivered this early?" Dominick asked the doctor.

"Yes, with her already past the 30 weeks mark, the baby would be able to survive outside the womb with no issues. The lungs and everything are fully developed by now. It may have to stay for a couple of weeks to be monitored for any complications, but there would be no serious issues with delivering now, no matter what. Both mother and child would be fine." The doctor answered, ready to head back to his patient.

"Go Highlander. She needs you right now. Put

aside all the bullshit, we've got both your sixes covered. We'll be here waiting for word." Dude said, pushing Highlander towards the retreating doctor.

"Don't show your anger right now. That anger isn't with her, it's with the people involved." Doc told Highlander from the sidelines.

"Aye, I will. She and the babe are what's important to me." Highlander answered as he left the waiting room, following the doctor down the hall.

Two hours, lots of tears, soft and hard words later, Highlander walked back into the waiting room with a huge grin on his face. "We have twins! One boy and one girl" Highlander announced to the stunned group.

"The fuck? Twins?" Cortez, Diesl, York and Raso all said at the same time.

"Apparently their heart rates were in sync. The girl kept hiding behind the boy during the ultra sound. The doctor says it's not uncommon." Highlander said, laughing and shaking his head at the same time.

"Is she going to be ok?" Sheriff Phillips asked Highlander, in regard to Pratt.

"Aye sir, she's going to be fine. They managed to get the bleeding stopped with the delivery so no complications or anything. They even got her arm patched up while in surgery." Highlander informed his fiancée's boss.

"Are the babies okay?" Wolf asked clearly worried about the effects of the fire fight.

"Aye, they both doing great." Highlander informed his friend. "Healthy set of lungs on them both."

Everyone laughed, patting Highlander on the back. "What did you name my niece and nephew?" Dominick asked above the noise.

"Well, we've discussed names for months. Laura wanted to name our son after me, but I was worried about Cody's reaction. Cody wanted to name the girl, if he had a sister. All names discussed beyond that clearly flew out the window when these two came screaming into the world. Our lad is William Fergus MacLeod and our lass is Rileyh Raven MacLeod." Highlander announced to the crowd.

"Love the names. I take it she insisted on keeping it as close to Scottish as she could?" Dominick asked with a smile on his face.

"Aye. There's also something we'd like to ask all of ye. Since our plan was to have the wedding before the babe was born, and that clearly didn't happen, we've asked the nurses to find a chaplain, we're getting married now, and will re-plan our actual wedding later, once all this shite has died down. I don't want another day to pass without her having my last name or my ring on her finger." Highlander informed everyone, causing loud cheers and clapping to break out amongst the group.

"Well, if you can't find a chaplain, Patrick can marry you. He got ordained to officiate a friend's wedding several months ago." Julie announced to the group.

"Let's do it. I would love it if ye could do it for us Commander Hurt. It would mean way more to us if ye did it." Highlander asked his commanding officer.

"What the hell, let's go get these two hitched before we get kicked out of the hospital." Commander Hurt said, smiling and shaking his head.

Thirty minutes later, two warnings, and a stern yell from Helga the mean ass nurse that they've overstayed their welcome, Pratt and Highlander were announced as husband and wife and the babies were seen by all. Photos were taken of the happy couple as a family, Cody included, as well as each parent holding a baby. Cody was also photographed holding his siblings on cloud nine.

CHAPTER 4

Two days after the twins were born, Raso and Cortez came to the hospital to visit Pratt. Highlander had been sent home by his wife to get some much-needed rest and to meet with the representative that had been hired to assist him with the investigation that his team was under. The three women talked about the babies, when she would be able to go home and how long the dr was putting her out of work.

"Okay, enough small talk. Where's the investigation into the guys who shot up Julie's store." Pratt asked her teammates.

"Always straight for the jugular woman." Raso laughed. "Well I can say we've identified who the guys are. They are with a local gang who was hired by an unknown source to go after the store. We defiantly weren't the target, but they refuse to say who the actual target was. The Sheriff is about to say screw it and go against protocol, to let the SEALs have a few minutes with them to see if they start talking."

"Yeah, Sheriff is fed up. These guys lawyered up really fast. Their lawyer is just as slick and slimy as they are." Cortez confirmed.

"Who's the attorney?" Pratt asked the two women.

"Rainer Liminksky" Cortez stated, rolling her eyes.

"How the fuck can local gang bangers afford Liminksky? That guy charges out the ass for his fees." Pratt asked, clearly not impressed.

"That's what the Sheriff wants to know. It's evident they aren't paying for his services, so that means someone else is footing the bill." Raso stated, confirming what Pratt and Cortez were thinking.

"Something tells me that those guys are either going to find themselves shanked or dead once they hit the street again." Pratt said, burping her daughter, while Raso fed little William.

Several minutes later, Cortez's phone rang. Hanging up the phone, "That's the Sheriff, we're being requested downtown. Even though it's not a human trafficking case, he thinks it's connected to the attack on Julie's store. Julie was downtown picking up some dresses from a local office that donates now and then, picking up the load, when there was an explosion. No one was hurt, but the scene does have a couple of casualties and injuries. The Sheriff wants us to help with Julie, until the Commander can be located."

"Shit, I'll call Highlander and have him help find the Commander." Pratt said, grabbing her phone and dialing Highlander's number. "I'll text you what I find out. Go, she'll need a familiar face in that chaos. I hate I can't join you guys."

"Take care of them babies. We got this. We'll call you and let you know what's going on." Raso said as she followed Cortez out the door.

A while later, Raso and Cortez met up with York, Diesel and Rameriez at the site of the bombing. They met with some of the on site first responders to gage the situation while they tried to find Julie.

"Hey Julie, how are you holding up?" Raso asked the shaking woman.

Julie noticed that Raso, Cortez and York were standing there as she put her phone down. "I...I can't get ahold of Patrick." Julie stumbled.

"We were at the hospital when word came in that you were here. Pratt is going to call Highlander and see what she can find out about where he is." Raso informed Julie. "Can you tell us what happened?"

"I don't even know who the person was. The guy said my name and walked towards me. His eyes started bleeding and he started grabbing for his throat. Someone grabbed me and pulled me away." Julie said, shaking and crying. "When I came back out, it was a nightmare. People screaming and crying, blood everywhere." Julie finished, looking around.

Raso's phone pinged just as Julie finished her sentence. "Pratt just messaged. Apparently, the Commander and Wolf's team are out in the field doing some training for an upcoming mission. Highlander is heading down to the zone now and tell the Commander what's up."

"Thank you. I appreciate it." Julie said, attempting to smile.

"Do you need me to call Caroline or any of the other wives to come out?" York asked.

"No, don't have her come out in this mess. I can just wait for the Patrick." Julie answered. "She's at work right now anyway."

"Okay Do you need anything? Water? Medics?" Cortez asked Julie, checking her over.

"No, the medics already checked me over. Water would be good." Julie said, absent mindedly.

"Hey guys, Pratt just called. Highlander found the guys, Commander Hurt should be on the way. He will be calling you in a moment when he gets a cell reception." York said walking up to the women, just as Julie's phone rang.

"Hello…Patrick?" Summer asked, not recognizing the number. "Yes, I'm okay. Raso, Cortez and York are standing here with me right now…okay hold on. He wants to talk to you guys." Julie said handing the phone to Raso.

"Hi Commander…yes she is definitely okay…no, we're not leaving her side until you get here…that's what we're trying to piece together now…yes sir." Raso said, chuckling, handing Julie back her phone. "Julie, your husband said for you to hold fast and that he's on the way. The cavalry is on the way."

Nearly an hour later, Mozart, Abe and Commander Hurt all showed up, running towards the small group of women. After checking over Julie over, then looking at their surroundings, they looked over at the three women who had watched over Julie.

"Do you know what happened?" Commander Hurt asked, taking charge of the situation.

"We're still trying to piece everything together. Julie gave us the best information. From what we can gather, Julie may have been the target since she states that the bomber asked for her. What has us confused is what he used." Raso stated, giving what information they had to the Commander.

"What the hell does that mean?" Christopher 'Abe' Powers asked, agitated.

"Well, from what she stated, there were no visible bombs, devices or anything in their hands to indicate a bomb. According to witnesses, the bomber called Julie's name, but had blood coming out of his eyes. Shortly after Julie ran into a nearby office, the guy just blew up."

"Like spontaneous combustion? That's total bullshit." Mozart said, shaking his head.

"Apparently not, Mozart. From all eyewitness accounts, that's what happened. I'm sure there was more factors involved, but right now, from what Julie, the witnesses and evidence looked at onsite by both FBI and bomb squad, no device has been found." York told the three men.

"Detectives, do you think the Sheriff and the FBI will allow Cooper to come out and look around?

He's good with this stuff. Local PD's tend to use him from time to time." Commander Hurt asked.

"I'll talk to Sheriff Phillips. I can't answer for the FBI, but if the Sheriff goes for it, he might be able to get them to accept it. Take Julie home sir. If there's any more questions or concerns, we'll contact you or you can contact us if there's any from your end." York told the group.

"Thank you, Detectives. We appreciate it. Please keep us updated on the situation. I'll have Cooper on standby for your call to include him." Commander Hurt said, leading his wife towards the car, followed by Mozart and Abe.

Watching the men walk away, Raso turned to Cortez and York, "Do we have any video cameras that can show us who this person is and exactly what transpired?"

"My understanding is SDPD is trying to get a copy of the video, but they are hitting road blocks." Cortez stated, huffing out a deep sigh.

"Why would there be a problem with getting the video? Do the cameras work or are they just for show?" Raso asked, sounding confused on the issue.

"Well, considering this is a place of business and they are supposed to have certain security measures, something tells me they skimmed back on some of those measures. Wouldn't surprise me that the cameras are one of them, if that's why they are hemming and hawing on the subject." York stated, running her fingers through her hair.

"Hey guys. Well the company is hesitant on releasing any video without a warrant. So, it looks like the Sheriff has to get a warrant or the local PD does, whoever is taking the lead on this." Diesel said, walking up to the three women, with Rameriez in tow.

"I thought FBI was clamoring for the control on this?" Cortez asked.

"Nope, they are passing the buck on this one since they are going off of eye witness reports that it was a single person that they were trying to takeout, not the whole city block." Rameriez replied, shaking her head at the information.

"Don't they seem to care she's a SEAL Commander's wife?" Raso demanded, upset.

"Apparently that doesn't rank since it would be a local issue." Rameriez shrugged, frustrated.

"Hey, why not have Pratt call that computer guy the SEALs always use, see if he can't bypass the bullshit and get us a head start, while the rest of them play their politics. If we can find out who this guy is, then we can start from there." Diesel said, looking at the others, then the chaos.

All five women turned when they heard footsteps coming up towards the group. "Sheriff Phillips." York said, acknowledging the boss man.

"Detectives. We have a major shitstorm on our hands. Bomb squad is going over everything but coming up dumbfounded with no device being found. Raso, you said that this Commander Hurt has a bomb expert that the local PD's use now and then?" Sheriff Phillips asked, looking worn out.

"Yes sir, Faulkner Cooper, goes by the call sign Dude on the Teams. He's the best. He's on Lt. Matthew Steel's team, sir." Raso responded, making sure the Sheriff knew exactly who they would be working with.

"Bring him in. Something tells me we're going to need all the help we can get." Sheriff Phillips said, before walking away to speak with one of the local police officers.

"SEEMS like you're still failing your missions Lidell?" Mystery money man inferred over the phone.

"Don't worry about that failure. They are still

idiots. They have no clue what is going on. These morons still have their guards down. They are assuming it's a terrorist attack instead of a direct attack on that bitch." Gerry Lidell responded.

"I'm not paying for failure. I'm paying for results. If your men hadn't failed in Texas, I would have already been well on my way to the rest of my plan, but instead, I'm forced to back peddle several months. You do realize this shit needs to be done and buried before the announcements are made?" Mystery money man said, clearly pissed.

"Don't get your thongs in a twist. You'll get your results well before the announcements are made on who the candidates are for parties. Your fucking name will be among them with a squeaky-clean background. You seriously need to get them pipes clean man, just because you had to marry a stiff bitch doesn't mean you can't bang something else. There are plenty who know how to keep their mouths shut, or just kill the bitch after you nut." Lidell said, laughing at his own joke.

"You're horrendous. It's a wonder you made it as far as you have without someone finding all those bodies you've got buried. Get this shit fixed I want those bitches dealt with. I may even take one to 'nut' before I make her disappear." Mystery man said, before hanging up on Lidell.

"Damn it Lidell, stop trying to pull the fucking tiger's tail. He's not one to fuck with man." James Franco told his boss.

Lidell laughed, shaking his head. "That pissant is a nobody who has everything to lose. He needs us more than we need him."

"Well, he has a point. We're three months behind schedule. The news just came on reporting of a blast, but they only report one death, a couple of injuries Julie Hurt wasn't one of either." Franco reported to Lidell.

"Son of a bitch." Lidell shouted.

"There's more too boss. Apparently, the police brought in Dude and those Alpha bitches from the Sheriff's department." Franco said, pointing out Dude on the tv, surrounded by five women.

"Well, well, well. Maybe it's time we added those lovely hookers to the fray, for free." Lidell said, laughing as he watched the remainder of the news cast.

CHAPTER 5

"I can confirm the bomb squad's assessment, there is no device here. Without the video, we have no idea what the bomber used or where to actually looked." Dude told the five women and Sheriff Phillips.

"Is there any way to push the request through for the video, Sheriff Phillips?" Rameriez asked her boss.

"We're trying to see if we can get a judge to sign off on it." Sheriff Phillips answered.

"Makes me wonder what these people are hiding if they aren't wanting to allow us to view their cameras." Diesel commented, while she surveyed her surroundings.

"I'm thinking they don't have the camera's working and they are supposed to, to keep their company in this building or something along that line with their contracts." Raso said with a shrug.

"I didn't think it was a requirement? Thought it was more of a preference?" Diesel asked, confused.

"Some insurances, depending on the company and what kind of company requesting the insurance, now requires businesses to have security cameras. It could also depend on how much the company is insured for as well. If it's found out they actually didn't have the camera's working, they could lose everything." Dude informed the group.

"But wouldn't the adjusters who come to investigate their claim have to investigate, including looking at their cameras?" Raso asked.

"Not if they have someone they pay under the table to ignore it." York said, catching on to what Dude was insuiating.

"Ok, ladies. Let's not get ahead of ourselves. Mr. Cooper, any idea what could have caused this explosion?" Sheriff Phillips asked.

"That's the problem Sheriff, there's no devices, no one saw anything in the person's hands, and no reported gas leaks. Something should have been left behind if he used something." Dude told the Sheriff. "Let me get with Wolf, see if we can't get in touch with Tex. I can have him do some digging in this area for other traffic or business cams to give you guys an idea of who to talk to, or which way to lean to get the information legally."

"Thank you. Anything that helps. How is Mrs. Hurt doing??" Sheriff Phillips asked.

"Shaken up, as to be expected, but she's are doing ok for now." Dude answering, shaking his head.

"Does Mrs. Hurt have any idea who this person may have been that yelled her name?" York asked. "I mean, it could have been a coincidence and there was someone else there named Julie."

"That's what she's thinking to, but no one else responded when they yelled out Julia." Dude said, running his hand through his hair.

"There's got to be something we're missing. Thank you, Mr. Cooper, for your help. I'll let you get back to base. I know this isn't a human trafficking case, but something in my gut is telling me that if I take them off this case, it's going to be a major mistake." Sheriff Phillips informed the group.

"Well Sheriff, in my years as a SEAL, I've learned to never discredit your gut feelings. Saved my ass and my teams ass more than we can count." Dude told the Sheriff, shaking his hands.

Three days later, the Sheriff arrived at the office asking for Alpha Squad to come into the conference room. Each team member, minus Pratt who was out on maternity leave, filed into the conference room, each one taking a seat and waiting for the Sheriff and Captain to begin the meeting. Each one had a feeling they weren't going to like what they were about to hear.

"Don't tell me, the company actually didn't have camera's in the building that were working." Diesel started out, before the Sheriff could say anything.

"Well, that's the kicker. They were working, up until ten seconds before the guy walked into the building. What's even more crazy, Mr. Cooper got back to me as well, several other businesses within 20 meters of the main office that he went into, their cameras stopped working as well." Sheriff Phillips informed the group of women.

"Are you fucking kidding me?" Raso yelled out, clearly upset.

"Jammer?" Cortez asked, leaning forward.

"Funny you should mention that Detective Cortez. Because one camera did catch what appears to be a device laid on the sidewalk just outside the front door. So, it not only messed with the cameras inside, but outside as well." Sheriff Phillips announced to everyone.

"Son of a fucking biscuit eater." Rameriez mumbled out loud.

"That doesn't make sense, why cover up what you're about to do?" Sgt. Helen Brocard asked, confused.

"So, we can't see exactly how he blows himself and the downstairs area up." Diesel responded.

"Doesn't make any sense though." Brocard counter stated.

"She has a point. If you're going to kill yourself by self-detonating, why not allow the world to see your masterpiece on how you achieved it?" Cortez stated. "Suicide bombers want the world to know what they have done, who did it and why. If this was a real suicide bomber, blocking the cameras and cell phones until the device goes boom doesn't make sense."

"What if this guy did it without realizing he was going to go boom?" Rameriez wondered.

"What do you mean Ramz?" York asked.

"What if he was told to block the cameras and the phones, yell Julie's name, get her attention and grab her, but someone else held the button?" Rameriez concluded to the group.

"But wouldn't they have waited until she was in his

presence instead of once she ran into the office? There was no debris, no shrapnel, nothing once the explosion happened. If someone else was pushing the button, there would be something left behind from the device. But no device or anything has been found. The jammer would have gone off by then and we would have seen someone removing it or going into the building afterwards." Cortez said, shaking her head.

"You all have a point. But can we one hundred percent say for sure that Mrs. Hurt was the target?" Captain Irby asked.

"No, that's the other part that is driving me fucking insane. We can't say for sure she was the target, just that they said her name. But, according to Dude, even she is convinced that there was another Julie there since she didn't know the person." Raso told her Captain.

"Shit, so we're back to square one with all this. Alright, this is definitely out of our scope, but we've handled cases out of our scope before and always did damn good. We're down one, so that's going to kick our asses a little bit. I can bring someone from Bravo Squad to cover Pratt's post to give you that extra manpower if you feel that you need it." Captain Irby informed the group.

"Actually Captain, Sheriff, with your permission,

Pratt's already called twice about this. You all know how she *hates* the down time. Granted, with twins now, and being home, she's got Highlander helping her out, plus his parents are flying in to stay for a couple of weeks, we could use her to help with the paperwork aspect of this. She's got that mad skill of reading between the lines that we don't have." Cortez pleaded with her bosses.

"And if he gets shipped out while this case is going on?" Sheriff Phillips asked, covering his bases.

"Highlander is on 4 weeks maternity leave since the military does honor that. Even if his team gets called out, they have someone stepping in as team leader for him. He's not going anywhere unless there is no other choice before his vacation is up." Cortez answered, without missing a beat.

"Here's the thing Sheriff, *if* and this is a big if, this is Lidell, being a Special Forces wife now, this effects Pratt too. She has an insight into the Special Forces world we don't. She can help us find that information or get us in touch with Wolf or Dude." York said, taking up the cause with the rest of the team.

"They are right. Pratt already knows this situation inside and out. You bring in someone from Bravo or, God help us, Charlie Squad, we'd have to take the time to read them up on the whole situation inside and out as well as the key players. That would eat up time we could have been doing what needs to be done to get to the bottom of this. Our gut tells us this is Lidell's work." Diesel said, stepping up next to York.

"Well, you guys are the best for a reason. Alright, Captain Irby and I will go by Detective Pratt's this morning and talk with her, and Highlander, and inform her she can help, with the paperwork and research aspect, of this case. That's it." Sheriff Phillips informed the group, breaking into a chuckle when the women high-fived each other.

Raso held up a finger as her phone rang. "Pratt were your ears burning?"

"Always is when I'm not at work. Anyways, I called because Highlander got a call from Wolf. We called in Tex to ask for his help on the video camera angle after we heard from Dude. Tex found something interesting. He's sending it to me now. Soon as I get it. I'll send it over to you." Pratt said to her teammate.

"Detective does your husband know you're working just forty-eight hours after giving birth?" Captain Irby asked Pratt, trying to sound irritated but failing.

"Damn it, she's got me on speaker phone." Pratt said out loud.

"Aye ma'am, I do. I don't agree with it, but, have learned it's better to stand nearby and let her do what needs to be done sometimes. She's doing this from the couch, as we speak." Highlander said from beside Pratt.

"Detective, did this Tex tell you anything about what he found?" Sheriff Phillips asked, hearing the conversation.

"He stated that he was able to find one of the cameras near the building that wasn't affected by the jammer that was used. Facial recognition gave him the name of a local gang banger named Jose Filiberto. From what he's been able piece together, there doesn't appear to be any device on the guy what so ever. He only had a bottle of water in his hands, which he took a drink out of, and then walked into the building. Twenty seconds later, *boom*." Highlander informed the group over the phone.

"How can that be? There is no device showing on his person, no device found at the bomb site, and no bomb particles to even piece together. People just don't spontaneously combust out of thin air." Captain Irby growled.

"I can tell ye lasses this, both my team and Wolf's

team are looking into a few possibilities. There were three new types of bombs that came out over the last year, that was never made public to civilians. One, we know for a fact is contained and it's not that. Both of our teams are looking into the other two to make sure it's not them. One we would have seen the evidence of in videos, if that was the case, of a second person on scene, but Tex didn't see a second person." Highlander informed the women. "Unfortunately, I can't give out more information than that, without permission from the Commander.

"Heaven forbid, then you'd have to kill us all in our sleep." Diesel said, snarkly.

"Hey boss, they've identified the kid from the gang we hired." Franco said, coming into Lidells office.

"Any word on what they are suspecting?" Lidell asked.

"As of right now, they are claiming the kid blew himself up, trying to take out an ex-girlfriend who had just broken up with him. Apparently, she worked in that same building and was in the lobby when he went boom." Franco said, laughing.

"Good, that means those idiots will let their

guards down again and then we can make our plans." Lidell said, with a loud clap of his hands.

"So, what's the plan now?" Franco asked.

"Get the men together, time we plan our next move." Lidell said, with a cheesy grin, looking down at his papers.

CHAPTER 6

The next two weeks had the SEALs and Alpha Squad looking at every nook and cranny they could find to figure out what happened and who had hired the bomber. While the local police and the news media had dubbed the bombing a lover's quarrel gone wrong, the others didn't believe it. They worked together, behind the scenes, to try and find a paper and/or money trail, with no luck.

"Damn it, this is driving me up the wall. Not only are we no where with the guy who blew himself up, but we still can't find a damn trace of Lidell. The fucker and his entire team have literally fallen off the face of the earth." Raso groaned, throwing her pen across her desk.

"There's got to be something found. There's no

way he's gone bye bye. Someone hired him to take out the Special Forces wives." Cortez huffed, leaning back in her own chair.

Alpha Squad, minus Pratt, sat at their desks, some turning their chairs sideways, so they can see everyone in the room at the same time. Alpha Squad's work area was that of an open floor plan. Their desks had two desks facing each other, with two team members sitting near them, with two more desks behind them. Rameriez and Diesel's desk were the first two desks you walked into, once you entered the Alpha Squad room. York and Cortez's desk were next to theirs with several feet between the four desks. Walking further into the squad room had Pratt's and Raso's desk with two desks several feet from theirs. While Brocard was team Sgt and warranted use of the office in the squad room, she didn't use it, instead preferring to use one of the two empty desks for hers, so she stayed connected to the team.

"What if Lidell and his team are using alias's as well as their benefactor's money to stay hidden? We haven't found a checking account in his name so far." Rameriez stated, looking around the squad room.

"While she's got a point, just because they don't have a US bank account doesn't mean they don't have an account. We can only look for US bank accounts. We'd need a warrant to try and find one internationally. Let's not forget what these guys charge for their services." Sgt. Brocard told her team.

"Shit, Sarge is right. If these guys charge millions for an operation, they could have an account in the Cayman's." Raso acknowledged.

"You both have a point. But let's not forget these guys are trained to stay off the grid. What if we're going about this all wrong? He's been AWOL for years. There's no way he's stayed hidden using his information. Especially not with the military after his ass." York said, sitting up straight her desk.

"I'm sure they've considered all that already and still haven't found him or his crew. Something has to fucking give here." Raso said, moving her chair side to side, making the chair squeak with each turn.

"Hold up, we still have the cousin, right?" Brocard asked her team, leading her ass against Raso's desk.

"Yeah, but that's been a dead end since we got him." Rameriez reminded their Sgt.

"Pratt made a comment recently, about having Dominick reach out to an old friend, who's a spook. Let's have her do that and see if they can find out some information." Brocard suggested.

"So, we're literally going to cross that line thin line?" Raso asked, scratching her head.

Just then, Raso's phone rang with Pratt's ringtone, Sir Mix A Lot 'Baby Got Back'. "Raso"

"Ras, it's Pratt. Caroline just called me looking for Highlander, but he got called to the base for a meeting. Someone has been following them and they need assistance pronto."

"Who all is it?" Raso asked, signaling the team to load up.

"Carolina, Fiona and Julie are all together." Pratt answered right away

"Where are they heading?" Raso asked, heading out of the building toward the vehicles in the parking lot.

"She said they are heading north toward Ventura and Baseline. They were in Julie's shop when they noticed a couple of guys standing outside the shop, across the street. Caroline said that Fiona thinks one looked familiar, so they grabbed Julie and got everyone out of the shop. The tangos followed suit, jumping into a black SUV and started following them." Pratt said, relaying exactly what Caroline told her.

"We've got this partner, calm down or you'll

upset Jr." Raso said, trying to calm her partner and best friend down.

"Just get to them guys. Wolf and his team are deployed right now, Tex isn't answering his phone and Highlander is in a meeting still, not answering his phone. I can't even get a hold of Commander Hurt to let him know what's going on." Pratt said, panicking on the phone.

"We've got this Red." Raso repeated.

"Damn it, I hate not being able to be there to assist, not knowing what's going on." Pratt said into the phone, on a sigh.

"You'll be back before you know it, just hold on tight. Let Caroline know we are on the way, we'll be coming in hot. If they change their direction or anything let us know. Get them back on the phone and keep them on until they tell you we are there." Raso said as Cortez peeled out of the parking lot, with the others following close behind.

Thirty minutes, one direction change and a plan in motion, later, the three vehicles all holding members of Alpha Squad got into place, going in hot. Raso noticed there were two black SUV's chasing Caroline's vehicle, not giving a damn about civilians as they shot out the window trying to take out the tires or cause Caroline to make a mistake and wreck her vehicle.

Cortez and York, having prior military experience, came up with the plan to put themselves between the bad guys and Caroline's vehicles while Diesel's vehicle added an extra barrier, allowing Caroline to get away. Caroline was instructed to head toward the base and do whatever they needed to do to get on base and let the MP's know that they were being chased and the local police were trying to block the bad guys from getting to them.

Diesel changed direction as instructed so she was coming in from the north, headed towards Caroline's vehicle, while the vehicles Raso, Cortez, York and Rameriez were in, came in from the south, coming behind the bad guys. Their plan in motion, the team gave the signal and looked for their opening. Pratt was notified just before they executed to inform Caroline of their decision and exactly what to do, so they could focus on taking the bad guys down.

Cortez sped up right up to the back-SUV's bumper, causing the passenger to hang out the window to shoot towards their vehicle. Cortez swerved to the left, while York swerved to the right allowing Rameriez to reach out with her hand and shoot at the suspect. When the suspect leaned back into his vehicle, Raso gave the signal to execute their plan. Cortez sped up more, after having backed down slightly, moving to the left. Seeing the path clear, she sped up more, getting side by side of the rear SUV. Raso, being the smart ass that she is, waived at the driver while telling Cortez to hit it. Cortez swerved towards the SUV, making them pull to the right, giving Cortez space to cut in behind the lead bad guy SUV chasing Caroline's vehicle. York went to work dealing with the SUV that Cortez just cut front of. Raso radioed Diesel to do her part, which was driving towards Caroline's vehicle, flash her lights and then make a sharp turn, cutting Caroline's vehicle off from the oncoming SUV. Caroline made it through the gate, causing a commotion, making Alpha Squad realize they were in front of the base in Coronado.

The rear SUV swerved to get away from York, only to crash into parked vehicles in front of a store. The lead SUV slammed on their breaks, with the men jumping out to open fire, not caring where they were. All six women jumped out of their vehicles and returned fire. Raso heard one of the men yell go after the women, not caring they were in a secured area. Two of the men grabbed a water bottle and drank it as they walked towards the women.

The man from the passenger side of the SUV yelled out, "Julia Lyttle, this is all your fault. If you only followed your father's orders, then innocent people wouldn't have to die"

Cortez and Raso looked at each other confused. "Did he seriously grab a water bottle and drank from it before yelling his bullshit?" Cortez asked.

"Oh shit! Where's the women?" Raso said, looking around. "Everyone, get away from these men."

"The fuck, Raso?" Cortez asked, confused at her actions.

"Their fucking eyes, Cortez, look!" Raso yelled.

"Holy shit, their eyes are bleeding. Fuck! Everyone get away! York take cover damn it!" Cortez yelled along with Raso.

Suddenly, the ground shook as three huge explosions took place, causing glass and debris, to fly through the air in several directions. Alpha Squad ducked down, taking cover behind their vehicles. Several seconds later, they all jumped up to check on the civilians to make sure no one was hurt. Military personnel came running from the base, guns drawn.

"What the fuck just happened?" York asked,

running up to Raso and Cortez, looking at the debris where the SUV used to be.

"Raso? Ye lasses okay?" Highlander asked, running up to the women, with the rest of his team and Commander Hurt behind him.

"What the hell just happened?" Commander Hurt demanded.

"That's what we'd like to know, sir." Sgt. Brocard replied, joining her team. "Is your wife and the others okay?"

"Yes, they are on base in the safety of my office, for now." Commander Hurt responded.

"Good, because we have some questions for your wife now." Sgt Brocard said, sternly.

"And why is that Sgt. Brocard?" Commander Hurt asked, getting defensively.

"Because, Commander, just before the tango blew his ass up, he made the statement that all this was her fault, if she'd only listened to her father. I would like to know what the hell this asshole meant. Luckily, no innocents were taken out with their stupidity. But it's now a clear case of them coming after your wife."

"And it's definitely Lidell who is chasing them." Cortez inserted into the conversation.

"How do you know that?" Highlander asked

Cortez.

"Because the assholes who just blew themselves up, not sure about the ones in the SUV, but the driver is a hired thug with MS-13. Recognized him by his tattoos, but the one who shouted at Julie was none other than Dobson Black. I recognized him from the warehouse in Texas when we were held hostage there." Cortez informed the group standing around.

"She's right about the hired thugs being MS-13. We have Demon and Palo being rounded up by San Diego PD back at their crash site. It looked like it was Omega that was riding with Black, if that's who the passenger guy was. But I don't see Omega, or any of the MS-13 guys being the ones to blow themselves up though." York said, looking at the charred remains of the SUV.

"I don't think they are either. I want to know what the fuck they drank though. Because it was shortly after they drank from their water bottles, that they pulled out of the SUV and drank, then they went *boom*!" Raso said, mimicking the explosion with her hands.

"Julie wasn't lying when she described the way the other guy looked before he blew up in that building a few weeks ago." Diesel said, shuddering.

"I'm inclined to believe both incidents were related. Search the sites to see if we can find those water bottles, I want them damn things tested. York, call the officers at the crash site and see if they can search those vehicles for any water bottles. Have them handled with care until we can get them tested, I'm not taking any chances." Brocard said, issuing orders to her team.

"Sarge, um, uh" Diesel said, pausing, then looking at the SEALs, then looking away.

"Spill it, Diesel." Brocard ordered sternly.

"Well, you know we have our own robot, Clayborne. He is able to test the bottles faster than the forensic labs are right now. He can get a basic composite of the chemicals to look at now, the labs would take days if not weeks, time we don't have." Diesel said, with hope in her voice.

"Diesel, Clayborne's information isn't admissible in courts." Brocard reminded her teammate.

"No, it's not, yet, but he can test at least one of the bottles to give us an idea of what we are looking at, and where to go while we give the other bottles to the forensic lab to legally get what information is needed for the courts." Diesel replied.

"Clayborne?" Commander Hurt asked confused.

"Yeah, Pratt and I named him that after York,

Cortez, Pratt and I built him. He can test items for chemicals that can cause harm, or in this case, go boom." Diesel said proudly.

"He's done? I thought ye lasses were still in the testing phase?" Highlander asked in surprise.

"You know about this device?" Commander Hurt asked Highlander.

"Yes, sir. My lass and her team have been working on this robot for about a year or so now. It also talks to ye while getting the results. If it's successful, it will be an amazing asset for both law enforcement and military in the field." Highlander told his superior officer.

"Oh wow! I would love to see it in action." Caroline said excitedly.

"Fine, where is Clayborne?" Brocard asked on a sigh, giving in.

"The back of Cortez's SUV." Diesel said with a laugh.

"You crazy bitches had this bucket of tin in the back of her SUV this whole time?" Brocard asked, laughing and shaking her head.

"Yes ma'am. Gotta be prepared to be able to test him in the field." Diesel laughed, inching her way backwards.

"Go get him and test one of the bottles. Have the

rest bagged, tagged and gotten to forensics." Brocard said, laughing.

Cortez and Diesel lowered Clayborne to the ground and pulled out a remote-control box that looked similar to a PSP game console. Cortez steered the mini robot towards the small group of SEALs with a shit eating grin on their faces.

"Ladies and gentlemen meet Clayborne. Clayb, say hello to the audience." Diesel said to the robot.

"How you doing?" Clayborne said to the group.

"Did this damn thing just repeat Joey Tribianni's catch phrase from 'Friends?" Snake aske, laughing.

"Yep, that's Pratt's doing, to piss off the captain in bomb squad. He hates New Yorkers and women." Cortez said with a big laugh.

"Sounds like a real charmer. Okay, so what can this bucket of rust do?" Snake asked, clapping his hands together.

Cortez punched a few buttons on her controller, "Make your girlfriend scream my name louder than you scream at spiders." Clayborne responded as he rolled into a circle beside Cortez. Everyone burst into laughter as they followed the trio.

"Smart ass little fucker" Snake mumbled, trailing behind the group. "That's Beatle who screams like a girl at spiders."

CHAPTER 7

"Alright, here's one of the bottles from the driver who blew himself up." Rameriez said, handing Cortez a melted plastic bottle.

The group stood by and watched as Cortez and Diesel placed one of the bottles into the display tray that came out of the robot's middle. The tray slid back into the robot, then started making a noisy sound as it started working.

Doc, Mac and Highlander started chuckling when they heard the song that was playing from the robot. "Is that thing playing the 'Wonder Woman' theme?" Doc asked.

"Yep, that's my little input there." Diesel said with a grin.

"Considering who ye all are, seems legit." Highlander said with laughter.

"Thanks" Cortez mumbled. "Okay, these chemical equations are whacked."

"Can I see? I might be able to help you out." Caroline asked Cortez.

"Yeah, sure. You are the chemical queen here. Hopefully you can make heads or tails of this." Cortez said, turning the device towards Caroline to read.

"Hmmm, this is an odd formula equation. I've never seen anything like this before. Can you get me a print out of this and I can look into this with you guys?" Caroline asked.

"Thanks, any help would be appreciated. I'll get it cleared with Captain Irby and then give you a copy by hand. Don't want this getting out. See what we can get figured out on this. I've never seen anything like this before." Cortez said, shaking her head.

"Caroline, what's your immediate thought on this formula?" Commander Hurt asked her.

"Whatever it is, it makes the chemicals in the ice seem like child's play. It's nothing I've ever seen before, Commander." Caroline said, shaking her head.

"Sgt. Brocard, do you think your captain will

have a problem with Mrs. Steel getting a copy of the print out, to help us figure this out?" Commander Hurt asked Brocard.

"Honestly, no, I don't think so, sir. But, I don't want to say yes then something happens with her saying no. I will talk to her when we get back to HQ, then have Cortez give Mrs. Steel a phone call." Brocard informed the Commander and Caroline.

"Lass, do ye have an idea who is behind this?" Highlander asked Brocard and Cortez.

"Well, Red just confirmed the two guys as MS-13 members, since she's dealt with both men in the past as a deputy. Caroline, Fiona and I confirmed Black as part of the crew from Texas. My honest opinion is that this is the work of Lidell." Cortez said, looking around at the carnage.

"Pratt says that Demon and Palo would never blow themselves up. I have to agree with her on this. Palo is too self-centered to make a martyr of himself. Demon was rising too fast in the ranks to consider suicide." York said, shaking her head.

"True, and what I know of Lidell, he'd never send his own men out like that, but how knows." Cortez said, shrugging.

"I don't know, what if it's whomever hired them

making them unknown suicide bombers?" Diesel suggested, joining into the conversation.

"She has a point. What if the mystery money man is tying up loose ends?" Snake asked, agreeing with Diesel.

"But that would push Lidell away. Despite his actions, he was a SEAL first and foremost. I don't think he would go that far off the block to sacrifice one of the ones you backed him." Doc said, point out the small details.

"Well, he did murder, or should I say order the murder of a couple of his teammates, men that he shed blood, sweat and tears with in the battlefield, when they said no to his band of merry assassins made up of spec ops boys." Rameriez reminded Doc.

"We need to find the money man and fast. Can you SEALs have your computer guy looking in to the dark web? See if they can find any communication or something that makes either one stands out." Cortez asked the SEAL group.

"Yeah, we'll pull Tex in, see what he can dig up by looking into Lidell and his team further. See if he can find a bank account either in his name or an alias name, something." Commander Hurt said, with determination in his voice.

"Commander, we'll get them. My team won't quit

until we do. No matter what." Brocard assured the Commander.

"I know. That's why I'm keeping it together, for now, also for my wife without releasing my minion of SEALs tearing across the country to hunt this son of a bitch down." Commander Hurt replied as he walked away from the group to find his wife.

Alpha Squad wrapped up the scene and headed back to HQ. Tex reached out to the team to get what information they had and what they needed his help with. After several hours of nonstop research, interviews, and conversations with everyone they could reach, they were no closer to finding Lidell or the money man bankrolling Lidell and his team.

Four days passed with no more incidents, which had not only the wives on edge but the SEALs and Alpha Squad ready to pull their hair out. Six days after the incident, Wolf, only back from overseas several hours received a phone call that an attempt against Rayne, Mary, Emily, and Kassie as made in Texas. Like the attempts in San Diego, the person blew themselves up. Luckily for the wives in Texas, they were too far away when the suspect yelled Emily's name and detonating himself up. Thankfully no one was hurt from the blast.

It was decided at this time that all three teams,

Wolf and Highlander's SEAL teams, and Ghost's Delta team were grouping together with Alpha Squad to end the threat once and for all, together. The Delta's drove to San Diego with the wives and children in tow, spreading out amongst the two SEAL team's homes. It was driving all three teams crazy to find out why they were being targeted.

Six weeks after giving birth to her twins, Pratt, against Highlander's wishes with everything going on, was back at HQ in full uniform ready to help her team kick ass and figure out what was going on.

"Detective Pratt" she said answering her cell phone.

"Laura? It's Rayne. I can't get ahold of Ghost. Someone is following us." Rayne said, trying not to panic on the phone.

"Rayne, where are you?" Pratt asked, jumping up from her seat, signaling her team at the same time.

"Cookie says 28th and Imperial are the cross streets we are nearing." Rayne relayed.

"Ok, what are you driving?" Pratt asked, running to her car with her team keeping in step behind her. She heard Cortez trying to call Wolf while Raso tried calling Highlander for her.

"We are in a black minivan that Benny and Jessyka loaned us." Rayne said.

"I know his minivan. Stay on the phone with me, who all is in the vehicle?" Pratt asked, jumping in her vehicle and starting it up.

"Cookie is driving, Hollywood is riding shotgun, myself, Fiona, Kassie and Julie are in the back two seats. We were helping Julie with some pick ups she needed to do for the shop." Rayne relayed, the panic starting to sound in her voice.

"Okay, good, you have Cookie behind the wheel and Hollywood there with you guys. Do *everything* they tell you ladies to do. This is their element. My team and I will help intercept you guys in approximately ten minutes. San Diego PD is assisting, thanks to my Sgt getting ahold of my brother Dominick. Cortez got ahold of Cutter, he's hauling ass to the meeting where the three teams are to get the men. Raso is on the phone with Tex as we speak and he's assisting us the best he can for now." Pratt said as she squealed tires around a corner.

"Oh God...*look out!*" Rayne screamed out into the phone.

Pratt and Raso heard tires screeching, a loud crash, screams, shouting, glass shattering, then eerie silence coming through the car Bluetooth. Pratt pushed the gas pedal harder, weaving in and out of traffic, sirens going, horn blaring, silently praying that when they got there that everyone was safe, while pushing to get to them faster. Five minutes later, they arrived to utter chaos.

The minivan was on its side, the back side door and the passenger door were open, shattered glass everywhere, visible smoke coming from under the hood of the vehicle, gasoline smell surrounded them, and one of the front tires still spinning, despite the tire not being on the road. Alpha Squad jumped from their vehicles and ran to the overturned wreck, screaming everyone's name.

Raso, Pratt, Cortez and York reached the minivan first, climbing up as best they could to the open doors. Diesel, Rameriez and Brocard ran to the front where the windshield used to be.

"Cookie, can you hear me? Hollywood talk to me." Pratt yelled down into the broken vehicle.

"Pratt, we have a problem here." Raso yelled out from the backside area.

"No shit! There's a gas leak, we need to get everyone out of this damn vehicle before it blows. How are the women?" Pratt yelled back, while trying to help York pull out Hollywood so they could help get Cookie out.

"Well, that's the problem. I only see Rayne and Kassie. I thought you said Fiona and Julie were here too? They are missing if they were." Raso yelled back, pulling Kassie from the wreck and lowering her down to Cortez.

"Son of a fucking bitch! Hollywood and Cookie are unconscious. We need medics now!" Pratt yelled out.

Alpha Squad had Hollywood, Kassie and Rayne pulled out of the vehicles and safely far away should it blow. Pratt, York and Cortez continued to work side by side to get Cookie out of the driver's seat through both the passenger door and the broken windshield. He was stuck due to the damage from the wreck. As soon as they got him free and pulled out of the minivan, shots rung out. hitting the roof of the overturned vehicle.

Pratt and York fell from the top of the minivan while Cortez pulled Cookie to safety, using the minivan as cover. "We need to get away from this damn car. Cortez, you return fire while York and I pull Cookie further away to safety then haul ass towards us. I don't want this damn thing to blow up with the four of us too close." Pratt said nodding at York.

York grabbed Cookie's other arm, nodded back to Pratt, mouthing along, counting down to three. Pratt yelled 'now', sending Cortez into action, firing her weapon. Pratt and York pulled Cookie's unconscious body to safety, praying they didn't cause him more harm. Once they had him to safe, they returned to the hot zone to draw fire, giving Cortez time to escape. The three women made it several steps before the minivan exploded in a searing ball of fire, knocking all three women several feet backwards. The three women scrambled to their feet, half crawling and running towards safety behind a building.

Several seconds later, the women heard multiple tires screeching to a halt, should of different names as doors were slammed, more shots fired out and then return gun fire. Rayne and Kassie were hugging each other, trying to keep each other calm, with Brocard crouched in front of them, keeping guard. Hollywood, Diesel and Rameriez were missing.

"Where's Hollywood, Diesel and Rameriez?" York asked, helping Pratt and Cortez look over Cookie.

"Diesel and Rameriez are assisting Hollywood, who's a stubborn ass mule headed male, in finding where the gun shots were coming from. He was under the assumption, until a few minutes ago, that you, Pratt, Cortez and Cookie were caught in the explosion." Brocard said, looking around her.

"Well, he is Delta, Sarge. All Special Forces are stubborn ass mule headed men." Pratt laughed.

"How is he?" Brocard asked, with a head nod towards Cookie.

"He took a good hit to the head when the car wrecked. When's back up arriving? He needs medical attention ASAP." Cortez answered with concern in her voice.

"Rayne, what happened? Can you tell us what all happened?" Pratt asked the shaking woman.

"Well, we were on the phone with you, as you know, relaying what Cookie and Hollywood said to. Kassie was trying to reach the guys with Hollywood, but no one was answering their phones. Next thing I know, Cookie swerves the van and we were rolling over then nothing. Where's Fiona and Julie? Didn't you get them out of the van in time?" Rayne asked, starting to panic as she looked at the van on fire.

"That's the million-dollar question at the moment." Pratt says, looking back at the smoldering vehicle.

Seconds later, Cookie starting moaning. "Shit, I do *not* want to be the one to tell Cookie that his wife is missing." Pratt mumbled to York.

"Laura!" Highlander yelled out for his wife.

"Fuck me running!" Pratt groaned.

"Eventful first day back huh?" York chuckled.

"Bite me bitch!" Pratt laughed.

Both women turned to where the yells were coming from to see Highlander, his team, Wolf and his team as well as the Delta men. In between the group was Hollywood, Diesel and Rameriez with two men in tow, in handcuffs. To their surprise, Fiona was found with them, unharmed, running towards their group, yelling her husband's name.

"Looks like they caught mice in the fray." York said, hope in her voice.

"Let's hope this jackass knows more about what's going on then the last idiot we interrogated." Pratt said. "This shit is getting old. They managed to succeed in getting Julie, but it leads us no closer to who is behind all this and why."

"Let's hope Fiona can give us some clues as to where Julie is and who the fuck is behind this latest disaster." York said, stepping away as Highlander got to them.

CHAPTER 8

The large group huddled in the waiting room of the local hospital while they waited for Kassie, Rayne, Fiona, Cookie and Hollywood to be checked out, against their wishes. No one was really talking about the event now, not wanting to rehash just yet. The two suspects were taken to HQ and put in holding until the women could get back to the office to do their interrogation. No one wanted to tell their Commanding Officer that his wife was missing, but Wolf and Highlander went together as they broke the news to Commander Hurst about his wife's kidnapping and what was being set up to find out who did it.

They had already received word that Tex and

Melody were on their way to California to help in the search for Julie and assist in any way they could. Alpha Squad was happy to have the retired SEAL coming to their aide. They loved that Tex could cut through all red tape and not give a shit. They already knew there would be no court room in the future the way this was going. This was a fight to the finish, and they were mentally preparing themselves for this outcome.

Pratt and York went into the back, following a nurse, so they could quickly talk to Fiona and Cookie. "Hey Fee, how are you holding up?" Pratt asked, Fiona quietly.

"I'm hanging in there. Thank you, guys, for saving Cookie. He's going to be okay, thanks you guys. I could never thank you enough, I know." Fiona responded, fighting back the tears.

"I'm glad he's going to be ok." York said, hugging Fiona.

"He's right here and can still here you, despite the whispering." Cookie mumbled.

The three women laughed lightly. "We wouldn't have it any other way Cooks." Pratt said with a smile. "Doc giving you a clean bill of health?"

"Yes, he's just waiting for two other test results, then we can head out. You find Julie?" Cookie asked.

"No, Hollywood says that she was no where near where they found Fiona. The suspects are back at HQ and we're going to head back there in a few to get started with the interrogation. We wanted to check on you guys." Pratt said, looking towards Fiona. "Fee, I really hate to do this now, but anything you can tell us before we go toe to toe with this guy? What do you remember?"

"Not much. All I really remember is this guy dragging me to another car, looked like a one of those white vans, yelling at them to hurry up. They were splitting up, one took Julie and the other took me. Said something about the boss man wanted Julie and didn't give a shit what they did with me. They were upset that they didn't have time to run back and get Kassie and Rayne." Fiona said, sighing on the last part. "I just don't understand any of this. What have we done to deserve all this?"

"You guys did nothing, Fiona. This is all on them, not you. We will get them. Don't doubt that." York calmly consoled Fiona.

"But at what cost? Julie is missing, he nearly got me. Cortez, Emily and Cheyenne had been kidnapped in Texas, nearly being taken out. None of this is making sense." Fiona fired back.

"Right now, no it doesn't. But we will make sense

of it. We aren't resting until this is finished. Mark our words, Fiona." Pratt told Cookie and Fiona firmly.

"Fiona, did they say any names, any places or mention anything that may not have seem important or just random?" York asked.

"Something about a Liaman or something along those lines. Then there was an ash man or something. I was in and out of it, so I only caught bits and pieces of the conversation. I'm sorry." Fiona said, sighing, starting to get upset.

"That helps. We'll see what we can piece together once we interrogate the suspects. See what we can pull out of these guys about Julie's whereabouts." Pratt said, hugging Fiona.

"Cookie, you rest, we'll see you guys in a few hours. We're heading back to the office to get the interrogation started. Brocard just sent a text, she's letting you and me go first." York said, putting her phone away.

While Wolf and Highlander were on the phone with Commander Hurt, Alpha Squad slipped out of the hospital, letting the others know they were heading to HQ and get things started. Once everyone was cleared at the hospital, they would be able to come to the office, they would inform Brody to let them back, so they could watch the interrogation.

Once back at HQ, Pratt relayed what Fiona told her and York, then outlined their plan of attack. They decided they would work into teams, Pratt and York would take on the shooter, who turned out to be one of Lidell's men, Edmend Jones, while Cortez and Raso took on the suspect who had been guarding Fiona in the back of the van. They found out he was just a hired thug that Jones picked up to help kill two birds with one stone.

"Hello Mr. Jones. I'm Detective Pratt and this is Detective York. You've been read your Miranda rights by Lt. Heil a few moments ago. Your accommodations to your liking?" Pratt asked, as she and York took their seats across from the suspect.

"You call that shit accommodations? I've been to hovels in the Middle East that are better than this bullshit. I'm not talking to you hookers. I want my attorney, now!" Edmend Jones snarled.

"Okay, we can get right on that for you. While you're contacting your attorney, we'll contact the Pentagon and inform them that your carcass is in our possession and that your AWOL team happens to be here in San Diego. Curious how well your attorney can help you once he realizes there's no pay out for him since you'll be spending the rest of your life in Ft. Leavenworth for three counts of homicide, your own SEAL brothers." Pratt said, shrugging as she stood to leave, York right behind her with a smirk on their face.

Edmend started laughing. "You bitches don't know shit. If you did, they would already be here."

"Well, actually, we wanted to have some fun with you before we turned what's left of your ass over to the Pentagon, so you can start serving the time for being a traitor to your country." York said, stepping around Pratt to head to the door.

"Well, that's her idea, I was actually going to let some real SEALs have some fun for turning your back on the brotherhood and tarnishing it's meaning." Pratt said, with a huge smile.

"Fuck you. You don't even know what it means to be a fucking SEAL. You bitch's wouldn't know about honor, sacrifice or the shit we put up with in the military. You're nothing but a pussy to warm our dicks with." Edmend laughed, slouching down in his seat.

"He's a funny man, isn't he? You know York, I'm sure I know about fourteen SEALs right now that would love to beat his ass. But, I'm thinking there's a certain Commander who would love to have a few minutes alone with this asshole. I'm sure we could turn the cameras off and let Hurt in here for a few moments and claim innocence when they find his bloody, beaten carcass." Pratt laughed, shrugging, joining York at the door.

"Yeah and his right to touch me would be?" Edmend sneered at the women.

"Well, let's see, besides the obvious fact you're a traitor who tarnished the SEAL reputation, there's also the matter of his pregnant wife you kidnapped at the same time you kidnapped Fiona Knox." York reminded the former SEAL.

"I never touched no Commander's wife, unless she begged me to stuff my dick in her, then he needs to take it up with her ass." Edmend laughed, wiggling in his seat.

"Well let me refresh your member dumbass. You work for Gerry Lidell, a bandwagon of has been SEALs who turned their back on the brotherhood. You losers were hired by someone to kidnap Special Forces wives yet failed in Texas. Then your numb-nuts team came home to San Diego and went for Julie Hurt, formerly known as Julie Lytle. Ring any bells cuntmuffin?" Pratt growled back, close to losing her patience.

"We didn't kidnap her, you stupid bitch! It was a rescue mission her father asked us to do because he didn't accept the marriage between her and some lame ass Commander who's shriveled up dick wasn't cutting for his daughter." Edmend yelled.

York and Pratt looked at each other and started laughing. "Let me guess, that's the party line that Lidell has you guys giving in case you're busted? Hate to tell you this Edmend, but it wasn't a rescue mission and your sorry ass knows it. It was a kidnapping, because Julie Hurt loves her husband and would never need to be rescued from him. He's got more honor, courage and bravery in his thumb than your moronic ass has in your entire body." Pratt said, opening the door and walking out of the room, York following close behind.

"Shit, the Commander is going to lose his shit when he finds out about this." Wolf huffed, hands on his hips.

"Wolf, you know the Commander better than we do, would Julie ever feel the need to be rescued? Is there any issues between them?" York asked Wolf and the SEALs.

"Wait a damn minute..." Abe started to say.

Pratt put up a hand to stop Abe's coming tirade. "Can it Abe. This is a legitimate question. We don't know Julie or the Commander like we know you guys. We have to explore all avenues because once we prove that this jackass is lying, and don't think for a minute we believe what he's saying, but we have to look into the comment's, so his attorney can't use that against us, *if* he makes it to trial."

"Sorry, I should have known that you wouldn't have believed what he was saying." Abe apologized.

"Not for a minute. He turned his back on what it means to be a SEAL. I could, nor ever, would believe someone who wouldn't hesitate to turn their back on the brotherhood, their country and wouldn't think twice about murdering one of their own." York said, staring at each one of the SEALs.

"Here's what has us stumped though." Brocard said, stepping up. "I can see the issue they have with the SEALs, especially if Julie was the main target. But I don't understand why they are bringing the Delta boys into the mix. You guys rarely have anything to do with each other. I mean other than Hammer and Highlander being brothers."

"Try saying that several times fast…Highlander… Hammer…Hammer…Highlander." Diesel said, to no one in particular.

Everyone chuckled, shaking their heads. "Leave it to you to break the tension without a knife." Snake said.

"I can tell you guys this, Hurt and Julie have been married for several years now. They have a kid on the way. If there was a problem in the marriage, Julie is the type of person that wouldn't have allowed it to get that far. She loves the Commander and he loves her." Wolf told Alpha Squad.

"I can say this, when Julie first moved to San Diego, she wasn't our favorite person. There was a lot of tension between her, the team and us wives. But we got past that, she proved how much she had changed through the years. The Julie from years ago is not the Julie we know and love today." Fiona told Alpha Squad.

"Why wasn't she the favorite person? You guys dislike her father that much?" Rameriez asked, confused.

"You guys know about my past, right? The fact I was rescued by these men in Mexico." Fiona asked, reminding the team of her history.

"Yeah, Cookie was the one who rescued you." Pratt said, acknowledging the history there.

"I wasn't alone in that hut. The only reason I was found was because Senator Lytle sent the SEALs in to get Julie. That's how Hunter found me." Fiona informed the women. "When we were rescued, she was a complete bitch, tried to get Hunter to leave me behind, whined about the trip the food, me being sick and so much more. But she moved to San Diego, looked for the SEALs to thank them for rescuing her and apologize for her attitude and actions during the rescue. She even apologized to me, has tried for years to make up she did in that jungle. Our relationship was strained at first because of the reminders, but she's grown so much since that nightmare. She loves the Commander very much, she would never want to leave him. She was so excited about the pregnancy and the fact she would have a small part of him when he's gone for the day." Fiona finished strongly.

"Okay, I can see why they would be after Fiona then. What if this is pay back for Mexico? Still doesn't explain why they would go after the Delta Force wives." Brocard said, looking at her team.

"Excuse the fuck out of you?" Cookie piped up.

"Hold on a minute Mr. Knox. Let us finish before getting upset. Please." Brocard said, staring straight at Cookie. "Can you boys tell us if the men who took the two women in Mexico are gone?"

"Yes ma'am. That's how Julie's mother was killed.

When her father threw a party in honor of my team and the fact his daughter was alive and acknowledging our marriage, the kidnappers decided to try and take out her father and kidnap my wife again. They were killed as a result of the incident in a black op sanctioned by the President by my team and another black op team that will not be brought into this." Commander Hurt said, stepping into the room. "Now, will someone tell me what the fuck does this have to do with you finding my wife?"

"Well, Commander, according to the suspect we have in custody, he claims that her father hired them to *'rescue'* your wife from you. Something about her not being able to get out of the marriage." York told Commander Hurt. "That's why we are asking the questions. We're trying to find something that we can use to get him to slip up."

"They did offer to give you a few minutes alone with the suspect." Dude told their Commander, letting him know in SEAL code that they are on his side, not the suspects.

"Diesel, what did you guys get out of the idiot that he was arrested with?" Brocard asked the other two women.

"A whole lot of nothing. He only knew they were to take the women and kill any men in the vehicle. He wasn't given any names or any other information. He was to follow the dumbass York and Pratt interrogated. He and his brother were hired at the last minute. His brother was given the instructions to take Julie straight to Lidell at a warehouse near Dead Man's Point." Diesel informed everyone.

"Shit!" Pratt, York, Cortez and Brocard murmured together.

"What?" The SEALs and Delta all asked at the same time.

"Dead Man's Point is part of a war zone right now between MS-13, the Russians, Albanians, Serbians, Jamaicans, Bloods and Crips. If they've got a warehouse in the middle of that shit, someone's got their eye on them already and we'll be walking into a suicide mission. They all know who we are. Bloods and Crips, we don't have an issue with. They tend to back away when we come around because they aren't that big into human trafficking. They are more into the arms and drugs side of things. But MS-13, Russians, Albanians, Serbians and the Jamaicans, well that's another story. The latter ones are still pissed with us due to an op two weeks ago when we took out several of their members, while the others have always hated us for putting a huge dent in their operations the last year." York told the men.

"How do you want to handle this Sarge? I can reach out to a contact with one of the Bloods or the Crips, maybe they can help us locate the warehouse." Pratt said, looking at everyone, trying to come up with a plan.

"Cortez, you and York reach out to your contacts. You gentlemen said your computer expert is on the way? Do you know when he'll land in San Diego?" Brocard asked the men.

"He'll be landing in about an hour and a half. He and Melody will be staying with Caroline and myself since we have some of his set up still at the house and we can use it as our base of operations." Wolf offered the group.

"Okay, so the deep stuff we would need will have to wait. Commander, I'm sorry but I'm going to have Tex do a in depth research on your wife and your father in law. Something tells me it's in connection to them." Pratt told Commander Hurt.

"I can get my father in law on the phone, so you can talk to him." Commander Hurt offered.

"No, don't take this the wrong way, but *if* he truly is involved, behind yours and your wife's back, I don't want to alert him to anything we've gotten. If someone is trying to use his name and frame him, then we don't want to alert them that we are on their trail. I want to leave the Senator in the dark as much as possible." Brocard informed Commander Hurt.

"My men and I are a part of every aspect, no surprises!" Commander Hurt demanded.

"Wouldn't have it any other way." Brocard answered

CHAPTER 9

Alpha Squad worked beside the SEALs and Delta's trying to piece together what information they could. Once Tex and Melody arrived into San Diego, the activity grew even crazier. Tex was put to work immediately working on what information he was given by those working in the field. Alpha Squad reached out to their informants in the Bloods and Crips to see if they could find out where this warehouse was located.

Commander Hurt finally called a halt to all activity late into the night. "As much as I hate to admit this, everyone needs a few hours of rest. We're all burning both ends of the candlestick here. Go home, get a few hours of sleep and everyone meet back here at 0800."

"But we're close sir." Diesel said, yawning at the same time.

"Yes, we are Detective Diesel, but you ladies are dead on your feet. My men need a couple of hours down time to recuperate as well after the events of earlier. Fresh eyes and bodies will help when we go up against Lidell and his men. Tex has his computer running and will contact everyone if it turns up anything." Commander Hurt said, acknowledging that everyone wanted to help him find his wife.

Highlander and Pratt entered their home, paid their babysitter and then checked on their three children, all sleeping peacefully in their beds. Both trudged into their room and slowly started taking off their individual uniforms. Pratt went into the bathroom and started the shower, taking her hair out of her pony tail and sighed. It defiantly wasn't her ideal first day back. Things could have gone so differently for them if they couldn't have gotten Cookie out of the burning minivan.

Climbing into the shower, Pratt leans her head against the shower stall wall, while the hot water beats down on her back, soothing the muscles she forgot she had these last six weeks. So lost in her thoughts and feeling the hot water on her back, she never heard Highlander come into the bathroom and slip into the shower behind her.

"Lass, are ye ok?" Highlander asked.

"Yeah, I'm just frustrated that we haven't found Julie yet. She's pregnant, alone and God knows where." Pratt murmured into the wall.

Highlander started massaging her shoulders then pulled her into him, her back to his front. "We'll get some rest tonight and then get back on the trail first thing in the morning. We'll find her lass. Have faith."

"I don't know what to think right now Joe. This whole thing just doesn't make sense. I mean, when we were dealing with the Sophie incident, I could believe that Emily and Cheyenne got mixed up in the attempt to kidnap her, but, not someone having it out for these women. They have never done anything to anyone. They are the most peace-loving women I've ever met. There's no reason for them to be on anyone's radar. I mean Julie, yeah, I can get the idea as a senator's daughter, but that's it. She has nothing to do with her father's politics."

"I know lass. We will find her. Your team will not give up, the SEALs will not give up and neither will the Delta's. The best of the best is looking for her, and we will find her." Highlander said, kissing Pratt's neck, then sliding down to her shoulder.

"Mmm missed having your lips on me." Pratt whispered.

"Missed ye too. Did the Dr. say ye are clear for everything?" Highlander murmured into her skin.

"Aye sir, she did." Pratt murmured back, leaning her head to the side to give Highlander better access to her neck.

"Cheeky wrench." He chuckled, as he turned her around, dropping to his knees.

Highlander lifted one of her legs over his shoulders and slowly kissed his way from her knee to just before her outer lips. Getting to the juncture between her thigh and her pussy, he nipped her, causing her to gasp then moan as he kissed the spot before moving towards her pussy lips.

Flattening his tongue, Highlander used his fingers to open her to him, licking from her ass to her clit, sucking on her clit, then repeating the motion several more times. He looked up to see Pratt's head leaned back against the shower tile wall, eyes closed in bliss. He stopped when he noticed her arms were crossed at her stomach area, just above his head.

"Lass, why are your arms crossed?" Highlander asked his wife.

Pratt shrugged, "Didn't want to touch you and have you stop."

Highlander reached up and removed his wife's hands from her lower stomach area, seeing the still healing scar from where the Dr.'s had to cut her open to deliver his beautiful twins. He lowered his lips to the scar and kissed her delicately.

"Lass, ye are still the most beautiful woman in the world. This scar does not turn me off. If anything, it makes me harder, knowing that this body delivered three amazing human beings. This makes me want to worship ye body every time I see it, knowing how beautiful ye looked carrying my children inside of ye. Never hide this scar from me again, lass. Next time, I will turn ye over my knee and spank ye arse." Highlander told Pratt.

Reaching behind him, Highlander turned the shower off and picked up his wife, carrying her from the shower to their bedroom, placing her on the bed. "I need to be able to see all of ye lass. I've been too long without ye. And it's my own damn fault."

Highlander leaned down and devoured Pratt's lips, kissing her as if she was his life line to salvation. Moving his lips from hers, he kissed his way down to her neck, nipping and licking his way to her shoulder, getting to that spot between her neck and shoulder and gently nipping, causing Pratt to gasp and squirm at the same time.

Highlander licked his way to her breasts, teasing her nipples while he used his fingers to tease and pinch the other, then switching before he moved down to her stomach, pausing to again worship her C-section scar. Finally reaching her pussy lips, he teased her, licking around her clit, never touching it, with the tip of his tongue.

Pratt reached down, grabbing a handful of hair, trying to lead him to where she wanted his full attention, with no success. She was weak with need, begging him to give her a release she's never felt before, growling at him when he chuckled and moved away from her clit.

Highlander flattened his tongue, licking from her ass back to her core, staying away from her clit this time. Burying his face into her pussy, he stiffened his tongue and entered her core, licking and sucking. Highlander hugged her thighs to hold her tight as he licked, sucked and nibbled her pussy as if it was his last meal.

Using a finger, he entered her teasingly as he moved from her core to her clit, licking and sucking as he finger fucked her pussy. Hearing his wife pant and moan his name, he sped up, determined to give her an orgasm before he went any further. Hearing his wife getting louder, he took his finger out of her pussy and fed it to her, to quiet her down, as he placed his mouth back on her core, fucking her with his tongue. In a matter of seconds, Pratt came all over his tongue, allowing him to drink her juices.

Kissing his way back up her stomach, her breasts and then sealing their lips together in a heated passionate kiss, Highlander slowly eased his cock into her wet hot core. "Fuck lass, I don't think I can last long. I've fucking missed having ye like this."

"Mmm fuck me hard Joe. I need you hard and fast." Pratt moaned, looking into his eyes.

"Ye are going to be the death of me woman." Highlander said, bottoming out into his wife. It was killing him to hold still to give her time to adjust to him. He'd gone too long without being in his wife. No matter how hard he wanted to fuck her, he would never cause her pain.

"Damn it, lass, hold still. I don't want to hurt ye." Highlander growled when Pratt started moving her hips when he wouldn't move.

"Please, I need you to move." Pratt begged her husband.

"Fuck" Highlander groaned, his forehead leaning on his wife's.

"I'm trying to." Pratt replied cheekily.

"Smart ass." Highlander chuckled.

Highlander started moving slowly in and out of Pratt's heated core, groaning each time her walls squeezed his cock, as if it was milking him. He went too damn long without being inside his wife. Never again he mentally told himself. He missed being inside of her too much. This pregnancy was hell on him, being so afraid of harming her with how much this pregnancy turned him on. He couldn't wait to get her pregnant again, but he wouldn't go so long without his wife, if he had to make slow passionate love with her, he would, every damn chance he was given. Fuck she felt good.

Highlander licked Pratt's lips as he started kissing her, transferring her moans of pleasure into his mouth, as he upped his tempo. Groaning when he felt his wife's nails scratch down his back in heated desire. Placing his forehead to hers again, he looked into his wife's eyes as he fucked her harder, nearly coming then and there when he saw the passion and fire in her eyes. The love he saw for him in her eyes, pushing him to the edge he wanted to hold on to just a little bit longer.

Highlander leaned up onto his forearms, looking from Pratt's eyes to where they were connected, watching his cock moving in and out of his wife's beautiful pussy. Growling when he saw her juices coating his cock he moved to his knees, grabbing her legs by the thighs and spread them wider to give him a better grip to pound her harder.

"Fuck lass, I wanted to last longer, but I can't. I need to fuck ye harder. I'll go slower next time." Highlander growled as he pounded harder.

Letting go of Pratt's legs, he leaned over her, grabbing their headboard and fucked into her hard. Pratt wrapped her legs around Highlanders hips as she grabbed onto the sheets of the bed, leaning her head back and moaned his name over and over.

"Oh God...yes...right...there...fuck...oh...God... shit...I'm...coming...*JOE*..." Pratt turned her head and bit into the pillow as she came, so she didn't wake up their children with her screams as she came, hard.

Highlander leaned down and bit his favorite spot on Pratt's neck as he came, pouring his seed into his wife's core, gathering her close to him as he kept pumping, giving her everything he had inside of him until he was spent. They held onto each other for several minutes before he rolled over to the side, taking her with him.

"Fuck, I didn't hurt ye did I lass?" Highlander

whispered, as he tucked her into his side, holding her close.

"No babe, you didn't. It felt perfect. I've missed you like this. Don't ever put me through this again or I'll never agree to get pregnant again mister. I'll have my tubes tied just to piss you off." Pratt grumbled into his chest.

Highlander swatted her ass with a growl. "Like hell ye will. I love ye Laura Renee MacLeod."

"I love you too, Joseph William MacLeod." Pratt told her husband, kissing his lips. With small bouts of sleep throughout the night, the husband and wife got reacquainted with each other two more times before grabbing another shower and then grabbing at least two hours of sleep.

The next morning, everyone met at Alpha Squad HQ. The wives were placed in a spare conference room with the children watching a movie the team had on hand for kids that helped them when dealing with families or young girls afraid to talk.

Pratt, Tex and her brother Dominick walked into the conference room with a determined look on their faces.

"Okay, everyone here?" Pratt asked the room.

"Yeah, everyone of us are here. The wives are in the other conference room with a stack of movies for the kids, snacks and drinks." Wolf answered.

"You've found something?" Ghost asked, looking between the three.

"Yeah, something that we should have seen after

the second bombing." Pratt grumbled. "Thank God it was Dominick who noticed it or we would have failed big time. Tex was able to help verify some information as well."

"Okay, what the fuck did you find?" Commander Hurt asked, slowly losing his patience, wanting his pregnant wife home.

"Okay guys, what do you know about the history of Saddam Hussein?" Pratt asked the large group in front of her.

"The typical stuff…Iraqi dictator, lived in a fancy ass mansion while his people starved to death, two sons as evil as he was." Diesel answered for the group.

"He ruled with fear, had an expensive taste for exotic things, was a real sleezeball and sadistic as hell." Rameriez finished.

"All true. Gentleman, anything you guys able to fill in that we may be missing?" Pratt asked, looking from her team, to the SEALs, to Delta Force, to Tex and then her brother before turning back to the large group again.

"Well, it's known fact he supported Hitler and Stalin during their rule before either died. He was a paranoid son of a bitch, always using decoys on publicly known jaunts through the country." Dude piped up for the men.

"There were some suspicions on mistresses and possible other children, but nothing ever confirmed, as far as we know. Plus, he hid gold bullion in several places around his properties, totaling several million in each hiding place, caused lots of problems for some military members who wanted to find it and smuggle it back to the US." Fletch stated, shaking his head.

"All of those are true. Okay, so Dom and I had Tex here look into a few other things once we did a once over of the video and saw something not good." Pratt said, looking at Tex and nodding.

"I have to admit, I never heard the story these two told me until I did a deeper research into some of the stories we'd heard about the sick bastard." Tex admitted.

"Dominick and I thought it was just bullshit stories ourselves when we first heard them. I honestly never thought someone would be as sick and twisted as these men were." Pratt admitted. "Wolf, can you please ask Caroline to come in here? She was able to help us some on what the chemicals were for the bombs."

Wolf left to go and get Caroline from the other room. The group continued to spout information to each other about rumors they heard on the deceased Iraqi dictator. Five minutes later, Wolf returned with Caroline at his side. Everyone quieted down and looked at Pratt like she had a second head.

"Okay, so the reason I asked the question I did is because this story is two-fold. Most don't know this story, unless you're a true historian and investigated both German and Iraqi history or spoke with someone that were close to both dictators. That's the one thing our father forced onto us, and this is the only time we can actually thanks our dipshit father for." Pratt told the room, looking to Dominick for a moment.

"Is that why you were so damn good when you were in Delta?" Ghost asked Dominick with a grin, shaking his head.

"It helped me look at things in a different light than what some people do, that's for damn sure." Dominick said, agreeing with his sister's assessment about their father.

"Ok lass, what are you saying that we don't know?" Highlander asked his wife.

"Well I'm not saying you don't know, but maybe never considered factual more than a mindless fantasy." Pratt said, shrugging at her husband "Okay, so let's get this party started. As said before, Hussein was a huge supporter of Hitler and Stalin. Now we all know Hitler died during WWII, but Hussein agreed with his politics, but modeled himself after Stalin. "

"That's pretty much known." Fletch told Pratt.

"True, it was also one of the reasons Hussein studied German and Russian, which wasn't a known fact, more of a speculation since he would have a translator. It was never denied if he didn't used them." Dominick answered for his sister.

"Besides the politics of Hitler and Stalin, that Hussein agreed with, there was an even bigger reason he followed Hitler's life story, which we will get into once we finish the backstory on Hussein. Now, it was known he had two evil asshole sons and *three* daughters with his first wife. There is rumor had a third son with a second wife, but those rumors were never confirmed, since she refused to allow him to be tested and claims he was a grandson." Pratt told the group, looking over her notes.

"Was it ever confirmed if he is alive or not?" York asked the Special Forces men.

"At this time, no. The family keeps a tight lip, but it's never been confirmed if he is alive. The Hussein family pretty much stays hidden from society." Wolf answered York.

"Okay, now that we have that family history out of the way, what the hell does this have to do with the Commander's wife?" Captain Irby asked Pratt.

"A lot, ma'am. Moving on, as mentioned before, Hussein was a paranoid son of a bitch who used decoys. What wasn't confirmed is he sometimes used the decoys to obtain mistresses. Many believed he was faithful to his two wives, but it was far from the truth. He had three mistresses he used on a regular. Only one, it's confirmed, that knew he was the real Hussein while the other two thought they were banging a decoy. All three gave birth to children for the dictator, two girls and another son." Dominick told the group, looking towards Tex who nodded.

"The two daughters were never acknowledged by the wives, even though they knew he screwed around and had them married off to men who treated them horribly, the stray dogs got better treatment than they did. But the son, Hussein kept him quiet, only the two sons that were acknowledged knew about him and accepted him since he was just as sick and twisted. Hussein paid for him to go to the best schools and college. The bastard even went to college here in the United States." Pratt told the group.

"Detective, no other children were ever

confirmed, hell they can't even confirm the one from the second wife. This is information that was spewed to get media attention." Commander Hurt stated out loud.

"Sorry Commander, what they are saying is true. I did a little more digging into what information they had given me. It never reached media attention because the widows of Hussein fought the media, denying the truth, claiming it was the ramblings of a mad woman who lusted after their husband. But the photo of the man Hussein paid tuition for is his spitting image." Tex confirmed Pratt's story.

"Okay, so he has an illegitimate son out there, what the hell does this have to do with the bombs that we can't seem to find after it blows up?" Dude asked, getting tired of the history lesson.

"A lot actually Dude. Okay, let's back up. We all know that Hussein idolized Hitler and Stalin's politics on how they handled those they deemed less than worthy to live. What wasn't mentioned in history books or biographies was a little project that Hitler had going on up until the day he killed himself. It was mentioned in a book by one of the Nazi soldiers who survived WWII. This asshole was one of the small few who served the German leader himself." Pratt told the group.

"Explain why all this is being discussed." Commander Hurt grouched.

"Yes sir. What I'm getting at is this, Hitler wanted to find a way to get the people he wanted to murder without having to round them up, put them on train and take them to the camps then later gas them. He wanted a way to take them out in a way that would be unsuspecting." Pratt told the Commander.

"Hitler had four renowned scientists and their families kidnapped from Austria. Dr. Diedrik Jergensen, Dr. Alarik Eppersiel, Dr. Friedrich Drofengham, and Dr. Geoff Claussen." Dominick said, saying the names in perfect German.

"Oh my. Drs. Jergensen and Clauseen were world famous for some of the things they discovered and created. Things we use in the labs today." Caroline said, in shock at hearing those names. "They died of old age in Germany though. I'm not understanding their significance here."

"They didn't die of old age, they were executed at one of the concentration camps and their cause of deaths were made up." Pratt told Caroline. "Each one of the doctors were married with children. It's known that they all had at least one son that practiced in the labs with them. Two of the doctors had a couple of daughters and at least one other son that was recorded in the registers."

"Wait a minute, you're saying they *had* as in past tense?" Fletch asked for clarity.

"Yep. The daughters and younger sons were kept away from the fathers. Only the older sons, who had been working in the labs with their fathers, were allowed access to their fathers. In fact it was expected that if the fathers were having issues with what was wanted, the son had to pick up the slack. If they thought the scientists were slacking or not working the way that Hitler or the Nazi soldiers felt they should have been, they either brought the wife or one of the daughters into the room, beat them and gang raped them in front of all four scientists and sons. They were vicious assholes where the scientists were concerned. In one reported case, there was a very sadistic Nazi soldier who had a thing for young boys, he would literally rape the younger sons in front of the women and men. There's been a few reports where he's killed the boys while raping them." Pratt said with disgust in her voice.

"Is there a reason for this part of the history lesson?" Cookie asked, pissed at what he was hearing.

"The whole thing is relevant, Cookie Monster, give me a minute. Anyways, one of the scientists finally lost his cool and demanded to know what they fuck they were trying to create. Basically, in a nutshell, they were trying to create a way to use the human body as the bomb itself. He wanted a formula that would not only further his cause of genocide, but to be used to turn his soldiers into unknown martyrs when they took out American soldiers, hoping to turn the tide of the war." Pratt continued.

"Only our soldiers broke through sooner than anticipated in the war." Wolf surmised.

"Yep, so when word got through to Hitler that we broke through faster than expected, he ordered all four scientists and their families killed. The wives and daughters were gassed while the men were executed with a bullet to the head. One Nazi soldier decided he was going to go one step ahead and helped all four sons that were helping their fathers escape. He helped them out of the camp and to safety. The soldier told the four boys to spread out around the globe and change their names. The rest, we know thanks to the history books." Dominick finished for his sister.

"Okay, story time was great and all but what the hell does all this have to do with my missing wife?" Commander Hurt yelled, having lost his patience.

"Commander it has a lot to do with Julie missing." Pratt said, point blank. "Those four boys who helped their fathers with the formula lived, until recently. Jergensen Jr, who became Gary Kraus, escaped to London where he died several years ago from cancer. Eppersiel Jr became Heinz Schmidt, escaped to Turkey, where he wound up working for the jackass leader who used Sarin gas that killed thousands of people. His ass was executed as part of the cover up before NATO could respond. Drogenham Jr became Gustav Zimmerman, who escaped to Russia where he was killed by a drunk driver. And then last but not least, Clauseen Jr became Redmond Berger who went back to Austria, where he lived until he disappeared a year ago."

"Still lost here Red." Raso chimed in.

"Damn these people have no patience to see the whole picture." Pratt said, shaking her head.

"Getting there Raso. Now, you know the story about Hussein's illegitimate kiddo, the scientists and jr scientists, what brings this whole thing together is the fact that Hussein's illegitimate son is alive and well. He goes by the name Al-Rhahed Hussein." Dominick told the room, pausing to let the news sink in.

"What they are getting at is the Hussein Sr. found out about Hitler's plan and wanted to use it in Iraq. He set out to find the sons but could never find them. Hussein Jr took over the search after his father's hanging." Tex told the group, getting to the point. "He wanted them to finish the formula that Hitler had their fathers work on."

"What kind of formula?" Caroline aske, confused.

"The kind that would allow a simple chemical to be added to a liquid and use the body as a detonator." Pratt said matter-of-factly.

"That's impossible. There's nothing that can be

used to do that. If that was true, we would have found that by now." Caroline said, shaking her head.

"It has been done, Caroline. You ladies have seen the end result with your own eyes, the same as my team has. There have been no devices found at any of the bombings, videos back up your stories, except for the first bombing where the cameras were disabled. The person drank something from a water bottle and then thirty seconds later, *boom*! You've seen the formula as well." Pratt reminded Caroline.

"Wait, the formula you guys sent to me is the one Clayborne picked up. The one we've been stumped over?" Caroline questioned.

"Yep, that's the formula that two world dictators have been searching for." Dominick said, nodding.

"What kind of formula and how is it been used?" Commander Hurt asked, sitting up straighter.

"The formula wasn't making sense. It's like some formula that is comprised of like liquid napalm or some other form of liquid explosive that gets mixed with an acid, according to the attempt of recreating it. Pratt and I played around with it a little bit at the lab, creating a mini explosion. But, since it's clear and going into a water bottle, mixing with the water, it's odorless and tasteless, so it's probably using the stomach acid as the detonator." Caroline informed the group, looking at each person before looking to Pratt.

"What the ever-loving fuck?" Dude hollered. "Are you sure of this?"

"Yeah. Clauseen Jr's body was found about an hour ago in an alley, here in San Diego. Dominick was the responding officer." Pratt told Dude. "He was stabbed in the neck with a pen that was still lodged there."

"Ouch, talk about being penned to death." Diesel said, trying to sound funny.

"We figure it's Hussein Jr tying up lose ends. He knows that 98% of Americans don't know the story of his birth or about Hitler's dream. But something tells me with the discovery of Clauseen's body, the verification of the video that Hussein Jr is in fact here in San Diego, they are connected to the bombings." Pratt said with a shrug.

"Okay, at the risk of sounding like an asshole, what the held oes this have to do with my damn wife missing?" Commander Hurt asked again.

"Everything sir. Hussein was hired of the failed attempts to get at the women. They failed in Texas when we got Emily and Cheyenne back. They failed at the attempt on your wife's store when their hired thugs were taken out. They needed to find a way to get the women. They were running out of options since the SEALs and the Delta's were on guard 24/7 where their wives were concerned. You guys teamed up with Alpha Squad and that totally put a kink in their plans while you guys deployed. So, they hired Hussein to come up with a way to take them out since they couldn't kidnap them to sell them." Pratt said, breaking the news to the men.

Choruses of son of a bitch, fuck and damn it was said among the men and Alpha Squad. Everyone let the history lesson they just received sink in before going any further. Finally, after several minutes, Wolf broke the silence.

"Is there anyway to combat this formula?" Wolf asked, looking at his wife then Pratt.

"Antacids?" Pratt said with a shrug.

"Somewhat, if the stomach acid can be neutralized, then there's a chance it can stop the detonation. In all honesty, it's not a guarantee." Caroline answered.

"So, you're saying having a dart with antacids in it, to shoot at the S.O.B. who tries to blow us up?" Hollywood said with a scoff.

"Yeah pretty much big guy." Pratt said nonchalantly.

"But it doesn't get us any closer to who is doing

this? Who hired Lidell to go after the wives and kidnap Julie." Abe said, bringing the focus back to the bigger issue.

"There is someone, but my sister and I disagree on this. Tex seems to take her side, but, she thinks there's something hinky with the paper trail, while I think the paper trail is legit." Dominick informed the group.

"More like he didn't like the person and glad he didn't run in the state of California, so he wouldn't have to admit he didn't vote for him." Pratt said with a wave of her hand.

"Wait, vote for him?" Who they hell are you claiming is after our wives? Dude asked, lowering his voice in a almost deadly tone.

"Evidence is showing that it's her father, Senator Richard Lytle. But..." Dominick said, getting interrupted.

"You're on thin ice with that accusation." Commander Hurt seethed.

"Commander let him finish what he was saying before you interrupt, please. Because this is something we would have had to talk to Julie about anyway. Tex has already verified the information since she's not here to talk to us. My brother is following the evidence, which now does point towards your father in law, *but*, while her father is an asshole, I don't think he would go through this much of a fiasco to take out not only his daughter, but the wives, you, your SEAL teams, or the Delta's and their families like this. If it was only you, the SEALs and their wives, then yeah, I would agree with Dominick, but there's no connection between Senator Lytle or the Delta team. That's the only thing throwing this whole thing off." Pratt said, sticking up for her brother against everyone.

"Okay, I'll bite, what evidence?" Mozart asked for the group.

"Before the events of yesterday, I already asked Tex to look up some information for me. I wanted to talk to Julie, but she was kidnapped before I had a chance to talk to her." Pratt sighed.

"What did you find?" Commander Hurt asked Tex.

"Apparently, before she was kidnapped and taken to Mexico, she was set to marry a prominent member of another family, someone named Brock Ainsley, who was following in his father's footsteps in politics. His father's name is James Ainsley. Word in DC at the time, and still is, is that Senator Lytle has been looking at occupying a White House run, with Ainsley having a key position that will eventually get him in the bid for the Presidential seat a few years down the line. Only problem was, Lytle, being the hardass that he is, doesn't have the backing like he thought he did. But, if he had Ainsley in his corner, then it's sure thing for him to get the bid for office. Supposedly, he had arranged the marriage between the two when they were younger, but Julie refused to participate, causing friction between the two families. Ironically, two months after Julie's refusal, she was kidnapped. As Diesel likes to say, the rest we know." Tex reminded the group of the rescue that saved Julie and Fiona.

"My father in law isn't the type of man do order his daughter kidnapped, then rescued like that, Detective." Commander Hurt growled.

"I tend to agree with you, Commander. But, like we said earlier, the money and the paper trail lead back to him." Pratt said, pulling out some paperwork.

"The part that makes him look guilty is the fact that he used his great grandfather's name, Jamieson Fowler, on his mother's side, to make some off the book deals, financially, as well as making a paper trail. But, being honest, despite all of that, something keeps tickling the back of my neck that says this is all a cover for something else. You're not going to misspell your own grandfather's name, and someone did misspell the name. That's why I wanted to talk to Julie as soon as we found out this information." Pratt said, looking at Commander Hurt sternly. "we all want the same thing here, the truth and the end of this bullshit."

"Son of a bitch. I never knew about the Ainsley drama. Her father never mentioned running for President." Commander Hurt, said, sighing as he leaned back into his seat. "Julie hates politics, one of the reasons she wanted out of DC." Commander Hurt admitted to the group. "So now what? What does this information do for us?"

"It does a lot for us Commander. It gives us a place to start." Pratt informed the group.

CHAPTER 12

A knock sounded on the conference room door, Brody walked over to Pratt handing her a piece of paper, then walked out of the room, shutting the door.

"Hot damn! Like I told you Commander, it gives us a place to look. Everyone let's suit up. Nero just got back to me, he's seen lots of activity at a warehouse that's supposed to be abandoned. Says he saw a black Lincoln roll in about five minutes ago with a snazzy suit getting out of it. Something tells me that Ainsley is in town." Pratt said, looking over the group.

An hour later, all four teams were suited up and situated a block from the warehouse, waiting for word back from Benny, Casanova, Diesel and Coach.

Once word was given the players were still there and the locations of everyone, they were moving in. Ten minutes later, confirmation was given, and they mobilized.

The four teams snuck onto the property where the warehouse was standing, slinking alongside the walls, checking for openings into the warehouse. Taking out guards posted along the way quietly, as not to raise any alarms, the teams advanced inside the warehouse.

"Ah so you do recognize me?" A male voice said, snotty in tone.

"Brock why are you doing this?" Julie asked.

You really must ask that Julie? I could have given you everything you ever wanted." Bock Ainsley replied, hate and contempt in his voice. "You could have been First Lady."

"No, you couldn't. You couldn't give me unconditional love or a life away from the spotlight. I don't want to be a Senators wife or the First Lady. I wanted no part of that life, nor will I agree to just sit back while my husband cheated on me with every intern that entered your office." Julie responded.

"So, you decided to slum it with a squid?" Ainsley sneered.

"Patrick is an amazing man. He loves me, flaws

and all. He's not slumming it. I'm living the life I wanted. I'm blissfully happy. Why can't you accept that?" Julie asked, confused.

"Because you were my ticket to the Presidential office. You were the guarantee I had that I would be successful, but you looked down on me, even though my family name is better than yours. What's wrong Julie dear, thought you were too good for me?" Ainsley asked with a laugh.

"No! Never, like I told you and my father, Brock, I would never marry for less than love. I've found that with Patrick." Julie said softly.

"Oh, Julie dear, would he still want you if he knew you were ruined. When I paid those men to kidnap you and sell you in Mexico. Does hubby dear know about that?" Ainsley laughed.

"Oh my God. You had me kidnapped?" Julie yelled.

Ainsley laughed at Julie's hysteria. "Well, if I couldn't have you, then no one would. So, yes, I did. Would have worked if your fucking father hadn't interfered and used the situation to his advantage in his bid for the Presidency. But no, dear old dad had to have his baby slut rescued. Making me the laughing stock of Capitol Hill."

"How could you?" Julie asked in disbelief.

"How could I not? Julie darling, human trafficking is a multibillion-dollar business. Of course I'm going to be a part of it. Being a Senator doesn't pay well, while the power does have it's desire, I need something more."

"That's why you wanted Fiona?" Julie asked Ainsley.

"Oh yeah, I had plans for that tasty piece of ass. But, alas, she kept escaping my grasp. Once I've dealt with you and those fucking SEALs, I'll take care of her as well. I'll take care of all those fucking wives, make sure they know what they really deserve. Women are weak, useless toys that men only need to fuck and then move on." Ainsley spat.

"But why did you go after those Delta Force men? What have they ever done to you?" Julie asked, hoping to stall him to give her husbands team time to find her.

"They interfered in a business transaction. Selling out one Delta Team was good business, then they had to fucking rescue one of the men, granted he's useless now, but to take out the other one who was milking that single cunt, what is it with you weakass women managing to snag men like that? The pussy isn't all that great. If it was, I'd be a different man by now. Singing songs, skipping through the streets, sniffing the same snatch every night. But I'm no weakling. My father made sure of that."

"Enough of this shit. Where's my money Ainsley?" Al-Rhahed demanded in his heavily accented voice.

"I have it, hold your horses Al." Ainsley chuckled.

"I've told you to never call me that. It's insulting." Al-Rhahed demanded.

"Oh please. You're nothing if it wasn't for us rescuing you out of that desert at Ainsley's request. You would have died as the bastard son of a whore and a disgraced dictator." Lidell responded from next to Ainsley. "You only have what you do because of him. Don't get so cocky."

"At least I didn't kill my brothers or turn my back on my country." Al-Rhahed taunted Lidell back.

"Nope, but that shows you have no balls." Lidell said as he raised his gun and shot Al-Rhahed in the head.

"Damn it, Lidell, did you have to do that?" Ainsley griped.

"Well, yeah. You said to tie up loose ends. He was a loose end." Lidell answered with a shrug.

A shot rang out, dropping both Ainsley and Lidell on the spot. Kicking the SEALs, Delta Force and Alpha Squad into action. Julie was untied and taken to safety by Alpha Squad, while the SEALs and Delta took care of the former Special Forces traitors, having been given the green light to take them out. The fight was over in a matter of minutes.

"Who the hell took out Ainsley and Lidell?" Wolf asked.

"Wasn't me" Benny said, looking at Diesel, Coach and Casanova.

"Don't look at me, I didn't take the shot. I was waiting for the go word." Coach said, hands up in the air.

"Sure as fuck wasn't me, sniper shit goes to York and Cortez." Diesel said, stepping back.

Everyone turned when they heard two sets of foot steps to find Pratt and her brother Dominick walking up to the group. "What did we miss?" Pratt asked innocently.

"Fucking Reaper and his baby sister. But we only heard one shot, how the fuck did you guys take out those two with one shot? They weren't standing side by side or even near each other." Ghost asked.

"Who said it was one shot?" Dominick asked, with an eyebrow raised.

"Son of a bitch, they fired at the same damn time. One took Lidell out with a shot to his forehead, the other took Ainsley out with a shot to the back of the head." Doc said, coming back into the group, confirming both targets down.

Pratt and Dominick high-fived each other with a laugh. "Getting better baby sister."

"The fuck she is. Stop teaching her shit." Highlander mock growled as he pulled his wife into his side.

"Julie ok?" Pratt asked Wolf.

"Yeah, Commander has her being looked at by the medics now. She's saying she's fine other than a headache, but he's having her taken to the hospital to be sure." Wolf answered, looking over at the scene.

"Alpha men! You guys never listen to us when we tell you we're okay." Pratt laughed.

"Get over it." The men said in union, causing the women to laugh.

* * *

TWO WEEKS after the showdown that ended the terror on the wives, they gathered together to officially welcome the twins. Dominick, Wolf, Caroline, Cookie, Fiona, Dude and Cheyenne were crowned the official godparents of William and Rileyh. Wolf, Caroline, Cookie, Fiona, Dude and Cheyenne were also added as honorary godparents of Cody incase anything ever happened to Dominick. Julie and Commander Hurt were also invited to the gathering as it was also a celebration of life, the fact they were able to find Julie and end the terror that was plaguing all of them.

"So, Highlander, when do you think you'll be having more?" Cookie asked with a laugh.

"If I had my way, Cookie, my lass would be knocked up right now. But alas, I'm not that lucky. She's told me I had to wait a couple of years before having another one." Highlander sighed, staring over at his wife with love in his eyes, watching her laugh with the other wives, and members of her team.

"She's good for you." Wolf observed.

"Yeah she is. I hate her job, because it puts her in danger, but I wouldn't have her any other way. Her career makes it easier for me to understand what our wives go through each time we get deployed. Makes me want to be more careful on our missions." Highlander told his friend and brother in arms.

"That it does. It's made us all more aware. Being a father definitely suits you." Wolf said, with a smile, looking down at baby Rileyh in his arms.

"She's already taken with ye. Why do I have a

feeling I'll be getting lots of phone calls asking about her?" Highlander laughed.

"This kid is going to be so screwed when it comes to dating you know that right?" Benny laughed.

Highlander, Dominick, Ghost, Truck, Fletch, Wolf, Dude and Cookie all growled at the same time. "The little shite would have to get through all of us before she goes on any date." Highlander said, darkly.

"And that, boys, is why our daughter will be a 50-year-old virgin, still living in her parent's basement or at a convent." Pratt said, joining the men, taking her daughter out of Wolf's hands.

"I can handle that." Highlander defended the men, causing all the women to laugh.

"Lord help me." Pratt chuckled.

"I'm praying lil Rileyh is another Annie. That kid is so freaking adorable." Raso laughed, looking over at Annie playing with the other kids.

"I was too. She's so stinking cute. Emily, you and Fletch ever need a vacation, send that little girl to visit any time." Pratt laughed.

"Don't give him any ideas. We already have one on the way, he may send both to you, so he can make more." Emily laughed at Fletch's hopeful expression. Everyone laughed.

"Ever think about coming back to Delta, Reaper?" Ghost asked Dominick.

"Some days, yes, but then I see my sister and Cody, the answer is no, I'd miss way too much here if I was deployed or stationed here." Dominick replied, smiling down at his youngest nephew in his arms.

"Dom, if you truly miss it, go back. You already know Uncle Travis would get you back in without any issues." Pratt assured her brother. "Don't use me as an excuse."

"Never, little sis. As I said, yes, I miss it some days, But I would miss you guys way more." Dominick said, kissing his sister's forehead before walking away.

"He's a damn good man. Delta lost a good one that's for sure." Ghost replied on a sigh.

Life was good again. Everyone was at ease, no more worries about who was hunting them down.

Until Next time...THE END...*for now.*

Author Bio:

KD Michaels has lived all over the country pretty much thanks to her nomadic ways. Being born a military brat but unable to join the military herself due to her deafness, she gave in to her inherited love of travel and has no problems picking up and throwing a bag in the car with one of her kids and just going where the wind blows her. She hails originally from North Carolina, but has lived in Arizona for the longest, working in law enforcement there before going back to North Carolina to be with family. She now lives in Virginia Beach where she caves to her love of the ocean and the wind in her hair. She's a mom to three and a cat which talks back and thinks he's a dog when he wants to cuddle.

Her Guardian of Hope Series page: https://www.facebook.com/Guardians-of-Hope-

Series-1604509269791748/?
ref=aymt_homepage_panel

facebook.com/authorkd.michaels

twitter.com/azcrimegrl

Special Forces: Operation Alpha

Saving Laura

Protecting Shane

Avenging Angels

Avenging Julie

Guardians of Hope Series

Angel of Horror

Standalone

Montana Gypsy

There are many more books in this fan fiction world than listed here, for an up-to-date list go to www.AcesPress.com

You can also visit our Amazon page at:
http://www.amazon.com/author/operationalpha

Special Forces: Operation Alpha World

Denise Agnew: Dangerous to Hold

Shauna Allen: Awakening Aubrey

Shauna Allen: Defending Danielle

Shauna Allen: Rescuing Rebekah

Shauna Allen: Saving Scarlett

Shauna Allen: Saving Grace

Brynne Asher: Blackburn

Jennifer Becker: Hiding Catherine

Julia Bright: Saving Lorelei

Julia Bright: Rescuing Amy

Victoria Bright: Surviving Savage

Victoria Bright: Going Ghost

Victoria Bright: Jostling Joker

Cara Carnes: Protecting Mari

Kendra Mei Chailyn: Beast

Kendra Mei Chailyn: Barbie

Kendra Mei Chailyn : Pitbull

Melissa Kay Clarke: Rescuing Annabeth

Wren Michaels: The Fox & The Hound 2

Wren Michaels: Shadow of Doubt

Wren Michaels: Shift of Fate

Wren Michaels: Steeling His Heart

Kat Mizera: Protecting Bobbi

Mary B Moore: Force Protection

LeTeisha Newton: Protecting Butterfly

LeTeisha Newton: Protecting Goddess

LeTeisha Newton: Protecting Vixen

LeTeisha Newton: Protecting Heartbeat

MJ Nightingale: Protecting Beauty

MJ Nightingale: Betting on Benny

MJ Nightingale: Protecting Secrets

Sarah O'Rourke: Saving Liberty

Debra Parmley: Protecting Pippa

Lainey Reese: Protecting New York

Jenika Snow: Protecting Lily

Jen Talty: Burning Desire

Jen Talty: Burning Kiss

Jen Talty: Burning Skies

Jen Talty: Burning Lies

Jen Talty: Burning Heart

Megan Vernon: Protecting Us

Megan Vernon: Protecting Earth

Fire and Police: Operation Alpha World

KaLyn Cooper: Justice for Gwen

Aspen Drake: Sheltering Emma

Barb Han: Kace

Reina Torres: Justice for Sloane

Stacey Wilk: Stage Fright

As you know, this book included at least one character from Susan Stoker's books. To check out more, see below.

Delta Force Heroes Series

Rescuing Rayne (FREE!)
Rescuing Aimee (novella)
Rescuing Emily
Rescuing Harley
Marrying Emily
Rescuing Kassie
Rescuing Bryn
Rescuing Casey
Rescuing Sadie
Rescuing Wendy
Rescuing Mary
Rescuing Macie (April 2019)

Badge of Honor: Texas Heroes Series

Justice for Mackenzie (FREE!)
Justice for Mickie
Justice for Corrie
Justice for Laine (novella)
Shelter for Elizabeth
Justice for Boone

Shelter for Adeline

Shelter for Sophie

Justice for Erin

Justice for Milena

Shelter for Blythe

Justice for Hope

Shelter for Quinn (Feb 2019)

Shelter for Koren (June 2019)

Shelter for Penelope (Oct 2019)

SEAL of Protection Series

Protecting Caroline (FREE!)

Protecting Alabama

Protecting Fiona

Marrying Caroline (novella)

Protecting Summer

Protecting Cheyenne

Protecting Jessyka

Protecting Julie (novella)

Protecting Melody

Protecting the Future

Protecting Kiera (novella)

Protecting Dakota

SEAL of Protection: Legacy Series

Securing Caite (Jan 2019)

Securing Sidney (May 2019)
Securing Piper (Sept 2019)
Securing Zoey (TBA)
Securing Avery (TBA)
Securing Kalee (TBA)

New York Times, USA Today and *Wall Street Journal* Bestselling Author Susan Stoker has a heart as big as the state of Tennessee where she lives, but this all American girl has also spent the last fourteen years living in Missouri, California, Colorado, Indiana, and Texas. She's married to a retired Army man who now gets to follow *her* around the country.

She debuted her first series in 2014 and quickly followed that up with the SEAL of Protection Series, which solidified her love of writing and creating stories readers can get lost in.

If you enjoyed this book, or any book, please consider leaving a review. It's appreciated by authors more than you'll know.

www.stokeraces.com
www.AcesPress.com
susan@stokeraces.com